Rinky's Adventures Part 1
The Cursed Relation

Kuntala Bhattacharya

Ukiyoto Publishing

CONTENTS

Sunday Morning

"Rinky, Rinky, wake up."

"What is it, Mom?"

It was a warm Sunday morning on a chilled winter season. Rinky had decided to wake up late and spend a lazy day. Utterly disappointed by her mother's attempt to wake her up, she peeked out from her blanket, with the least desire to open her eyes.

"Your phone is ringing since long; I think almost 5 times."

"Let it be, Mom. I will check out later. Let me sleep."

"Ok, as you wish. I thought there might be some emergency. The number is unknown though."

Rinky's mother, Mrs. Khanna, just stepped out of her room, when the phone rang again.

"Again, do you want to check Rinky?"

Almost unwillingly Rinky replied, "Is it the same number, Mom?"

Mrs. Khanna stepped in again and picked up the phone from the study table of her daughter.

"Same number", she answered.

"Seems real emergency. Sleep gone on a Sunday. Pity me. Can you please hand over the phone, Mom."

"Sure! here you go, dear. You finish the call, meanwhile I will get you some tea," Mrs. Khanna left Rinky's room.

Rinky went on answering to the phone, "Hello".

"Hello Ma'am. Are you Rinky Khanna?" A female voice answered in a soft tone. Rinky tried to guess the voice, seemed panic-stricken.

"Yes, I am. Who is it? You have been calling multiple times. Is there any emergency?"

"Sorry Ma'am. I felt time is ticking out. So, I had to call you. Need your help urgently. Can I meet you, please?"

"Yes, you can meet. But who are you? And why do you want to meet me?"

"Ma'am, I will tell you everything after I meet you. It's very risky for me to speak in phone. Please understand and consider my request."

"Ok, I am texting you, my address. Are you coming over today?" Rinky inquired.

"Thank you and yes Ma'am. Can I come at 11 AM?" The voice on the other end of the phone sounded inquisitive.

"Should be fine. But what's your name? Send me a picture of yours so that I identify you when you arrive, your photo when you start from your place. And if you don't, I cannot let you inside my house."

"Thanks a lot, Ma'am. My name is Anu Srivastava. I am sending you my photo in few minutes."

Rinky hang up the phone.

"Mom, a girl or a lady I don't know, will come at 11."

"Oh, is it the phone call? Come have your tea," Mrs. Khanna handed over the cup to Rinky.

"Yes, not willing to speak anything on phone. Spoke about some risk. I asked for her photograph, name I have. Want to perform a search before she arrives."

Rinky sipped on her tea and stared across the window overlooking the beautiful garden curated with care by her mother.

Based out of Mumbai, Rinky had started her career as a journalist and was working with a renowned news group. While working, she realized her interest in scrutiny, analysis and investigations for various issues, some even related to crimes. Her interest was granted due attention and respect and she was shifted to the investigation and research department of the group she was working with. She continued working in the department for 3 more years, undertook several risks, gained many acquaintances, and acquired humongous experiences; solely because of her sheer hard work, dedication, brilliant will power, intelligence, and colossal analytical ability. When she decided to quit and start her own private practice, the leadership of the news group was very reluctant. After much persuasion, they agreed and on a small condition that she would assist them as a consultant when in need. That was her steppingstone to the world of private investigation. She converted the study in her house, that belonged to her father, into her office.

Rinky's father, Mr. Khanna, had left for his heavenly abode, about 2 years ago. The thought that her father did not survive to watch his daughter establish herself as a private investigator, depressed her for long. But then she realized it was her father's wish that one day she would open up a consultancy or a firm on her own. He was always proud of his daughter and encouraged her in every step of her professional journey. And hence with all the support from her mother, Rinky started her firm. She was 27 years old then. She put up a board with her name in front of her house and circulated about her initiative within her known associates and contacts. Being in the journalist arena, she was well-known, and many knew about her credibility.

Rinky's parents had settled in Mumbai, pursuing their professional lives. Her father was a retired IAS officer, serving the Indian government.

Rinky's mother, Mrs. Khanna, was a retired Professor in English. Rinky always felt her mother was sharp and intelligent, a trait she picked up from her childhood. Her mother was her constant support and companion in the investigations. Every day, after finishing her work, she spent at least 1 to 2 hours' time discussing with her mother. Being at the nascent level of her career, and the type of profession she was involved in, it was difficult to rely on outsiders. Though she had some trusted people to extract certain information, crucial sometimes for her investigations, yet she kept her discussions about the clues and suspicions, solely confined with her mother.

Sunday breakfast and lunch were always special at the Khanna house. Mrs. Khanna had employed a cook years back, but on Sundays she preferred preparing the dishes herself. And as per Rinky, those were far more delicious than the food prepared by the cook. After the demise of Mr. Khanna, for one- or two-months things were in doldrums. But slowly both mother and daughter recovered from the grief and re-instated their regular life, the way Rinky's father wanted them to be.

Today's breakfast was Indian Puri and Sabji, Rinky's favorite.

"Rinky, a small bit of advice for you," Mrs. Khanna started to speak as both mother and daughter delightfully munched on the Puris.

"Yes, Mom. What is it?"

"As a private investigator, it is very important to gain the trust and confidence of the people who approach you. There may be situations when people might be in trouble and would want to discuss urgently and even in secrecy. Certain sacrifices you need to undergo which may sometimes disappoint you or may snatch away your leisure but remember that may eventually turn out to be a boon in your career."

"Understood, Mom. Repeated phone calls are an indication of some problem. I should have attended to it, earlier."

"Yes, you are correct. The girl or lady might be desperate and seeking your help. Maybe she has no one to discuss her problem."

"You are correct, Mom. My bad I focused on my sleep instead of realizing the person in trouble."

Rinky's phone beeped with a message in her WhatsApp. She unlocked her phone to check.

"She has sent her photo, Anu Srivastava. Let me quickly check her details, before she comes in."

"Ok dear. You carry on. Let me continue my work in the kitchen," Mrs. Khanna picked up the breakfast dishes and cleared the table.

Rinky started walking towards her study.

The house was a duplex, well planned and beautified with care by both Rinky's parents. Further the lawn, the front and terrace garden enhanced the charm of the house, much appreciated in the neighborhood. Both the kitchen and the study were in the lower floor.

As Rinky continued towards her study, she felt another change in her life. No holidays for her now. She has to come out of the mode of weekend holidays, unlike her regular office life. And she was ready for this conversion.

Regaining all her concentration, shrugging off all the lethargy and morning hang-over, she entered her study and sat in front of her laptop. She had earlier transferred the photo of Anu Srivastava into her email for the detailed search.

She checked her watch for the time. It was 10 AM, she had almost an hour to prepare herself before the meet.

She searched in all social media platforms, and in all the search engines. Did not seem to be a high-profile person, but a commoner dwelling in Andheri. There were photos of her travelling in the local trains, beaches, Marine drive, and none of the snaps appeared to be suspicious. Besides, all her photos were public except few.

Only two things caught her attention.

One was her recent change in job as a personal assistant for someone renowned in Mumbai, but the name was masked. And another was, few recent photographs seemed to be hidden from public or deleted.

Rinky also checked that Anu was in a relation but was not married. From her birth date, she is supposed to be 24 years old. Question was, how did she know Rinky's number and why does she want to connect with a private investigator and not police when she is in trouble. For a commoner, it is normal to contact police, unless there is some big mystery.

With several questions in mind, Rinky checked the time.

10:59 AM.

Any moment, Anu will be at her house.

The Visitor

It was around 11:10 AM when the front doorbell rang.

Rinky insisted to open the door herself and asked her mother to notice the visitor as an external observer, as she will be busy engaged speaking.

"Good Morning Ma'am. I am Anu. It was me who called you today."

"Hi Anu. Rinky here", Rinky extended her hand for a greet.

And as she did so, she quickly glanced at Anu's face, hands, attire and at her sandals.

Anu's looks matched with the one she had seen on Facebook. The photograph of hers she had earlier sent to Rinky too matched - the same 3 rings she had clipped on her ears, common among young girls these days. She had few bangles, the junk ones, on her left hand and a watch on her right hand. Her dress was a t-shirt dark blue in color with few modern patterns and faded blue jeans, the funky style one. She wore a flat covered sandal, with a mix of blue and white combo. Overall, Rinky felt she had a fair sense of fashion which appeared to be a hint that she is connected with some fashion celebrity or maybe some actor or actress.

Anu, with a little bit of hesitation, extended her hand towards Rinky for the greet.

"Please come in, Anu. Hope you don't mind addressing by your name, as you seem to be younger than me."

"Sure Ma'am. I am very much thankful that you agreed to meet me."

Rinky ushered Anu into the house and towards the study. She sat at her desk and Anu on the chair in front of the desk.

"Do you want some tea or coffee?" Rinky asked.

"No Ma'am thank you. Some water will do." Anu replied.

"Sure". Rinky picked up a glass from a small closet near her desk, poured some water into it and placed in front of Anu.

Anu took few sips of water and as she did so, Rinky silently observed her without showing off her curious look as that may place Anu completely out off guard. Rinky felt an anxiety hovering around Anu, as her hands were not quite steady while holding the glass of water. In fact she was sipping the water with some bit of nervousness.

"So, Anu, what brings you here. What is the emergency? And why were you in such a hurry to meet me today itself?"

"Ma'am, can you please close the door of this room. I understand your house is safe, but I want to be extra careful before sharing my worry with you."

"Sure, sure Anu. That's absolutely fine. Let me close the door."

Rinky closed the door, came back to her desk, and secretly switched on the small transmitter beneath her desk, defeating the attention of Anu. The transmitter was a covert listening device she had implanted underneath her desk. Through the device, Rinky's mother can listen to the conversations with the help of another end of the transmitter which she keeps with her the moment her daughter starts speaking with any client.

"You can carry on, Anu. I can assure you that no one will be able to listen to our conversations and moreover my maids are also not at home. So not to worry."

"Thank you, Ma'am. It's about a tragic death of an eminent actress that you may have watched in TV 5 days ago."

"About Archana Gokhale?"

"Yes Ma'am. I was her personal assistant for the last one year. She was a very nice human being and I am completely shattered by her demise."

"The police have confirmed her death to be a suicide, right?"

"Yes true, Ma'am. But I know it is not. She was a lively person with dreams of owning a production house and earning worldwide fame. How can she commit a suicide? I am finding it tough to agree with the investigations. And that's the sole reason I am approaching you. I don't know much about the formalities of how you can be involved. But it's my humble request, if you kindly consider this case. Being with her for one year, I have learnt so much and she was more a friend than an employer. I really want to seek justice for her."

Anu's voice almost choked as she uttered out the words.

"Exactly, what is your apprehension, Anu? You do not think she committed suicide. Then what?" Rinky looked at her quite inquisitively.

Anu lowered her voice further and answered, "I feel she was murdered. But it's my humble request, please do not tell anyone that it's my apprehension. I am very worried I may fall into trouble. Somehow through your acquaintances if you consider investigating the case, I will be obliged. I don't know about your fees but will definitely try to compensate with my meagre salary. Being associated with Ms. Gokhale, I had a special bonding with her and feel disturbed about the news of her suicide floating everywhere. Request your help please Ma'am."

Rinky took a deep breath.

"Well Anu. I am sorry I cannot promise that. It's a government case and tough to sneak from outside. But I will try my best. So, in case I get through I will inform you immediately. But nevertheless, if you are fine, can I ask few questions?"

"Sure Ma'am. I will be happy to answer all your questions."

"That's good. Thank you. So how long have you been working for Ms. Gokhale? Who were her close associates? What was her daily schedule? And whom do you live with, or do you stay alone and where?"

"Ma'am I have been working for almost one and half years with Archana Ma'am. Her close associates were her bestie Ms. Dimple Ahuja, and her school friend Mr. Tony D'Souza. She had a full-time maid who used to stay at the servant house attached to her apartment. Her parents sometimes visited her maybe once in 6 months, stay for 1 week or so and then return back to their home. And surprisingly she became very close with me too, sharing all her daily engagements with various people, about her ambitions, and her future plans. She even confided with me about the people whom she liked or disliked. She was an early riser, woke up at 6 AM every morning. Oh yes, she had a personal fitness instructor at the gym nearby her apartment and was a regular there. I used to reach her office, a room insider her apartment, at about 9:30 AM where I had to brief her about the meetings, appointments, film and photo shoots, travels, and any other programs. Sometimes I had to accompany her in the meetings, else I remained in the office working on her activities and schedules, attending calls for her."

"Which gym did she go to? Can you give me the name and address? And also, the name of the fitness instructor? By the way, you missed answering one of my questions?" Rinky looked at Anu with a smiling face.

"Oh, I am sorry Ma'am. I stay alone but my boyfriend sometimes comes and stays with me during his trips to the city. The name of the gym where Archana Ma'am frequented to is "The DreamZone". I don't know the name of the instructor, but I can try to figure it out and inform you."

"Great, thanks Anu. Also, can you help with the name of your boyfriend."

Anu smiled, "You can eliminate him from the list of suspects. Though he runs a big restaurant in Goa, yet he is such an introvert. Seldom he speaks with strangers and with Archana Ma'am, you will be surprised to know he did not even visit her once; even though I insisted multiple times. He loves a simple life and is completely against the high-end societal group of people like celebrities, rich business people and so on and so forth."

"You never know, Anu. Remember, you are speaking to a detective. In my list all are suspects, and I am sorry that includes you too. You must be open-minded in sharing all the information you know and what I ask, else I will not be able to help you. So, if you can please tell me his name and another very important question, from where did you get my phone number?"

"I am sorry Ma'am. I understand. His name is Jose Branco, a Goanese guy. About me knowing your phone number, I had passed by your house many times. Well, my intention of looking at the board hanging outside your house was not to save your phone number but mainly because the décor is unique and very attractive," Anu smiled.

"Ok, that was smart and quick thinking," Rinky smiled back too.

"Ma'am, I should leave now. I know it's a Sunday, almost 1:30 PM and you must be late for lunch. But please try, I will be extremely grateful. I am an ordinary girl, with no reach to the higher society. But at least as her dedicated employee, I can try to rest her soul in peace. She cannot commit suicide, its simply impossible."

"I will try my best, Anu. Let me check out how can I intrude into the investigation."

Rinky accompanied Anu till the front door. She then came back to her study, carefully arranged the notes of the conversation, and switched off the transmitter. Her next act was to discuss with her mother as Mrs. Khanna had already heard the conversation and might have some viewpoints or suggestions. She came out of her study and went towards the kitchen. The time being 1:30 PM, her mother must be busy arranging for lunch.

"Hey Mom, hope you have heard the conversation between me and Anu."

"Yes, I did dear. She has left right?"

"Yes Mom."

"Now you go and have your shower. Its late. Let's talk over lunch."

"Sure Mom, as you wish. I will be back in 10 minutes. But we need to be fast in our decision, seems there is less time."

Mrs. Khanna nodded in agreement, while Rinky rushed upstairs for a shower.

Starting Point

"I am in a little bit of dilemma, Mom. This entire suicide investigation and analysis has been conducted by the detectives of the Mumbai Police Department and the Crime Department. Re-investigating the case will be challenging and I may have to face many hurdles and may even be prevented to intrude into it. On the other hand, whether to rely on what Anu has referred, her doubts and concerns and her request. What's your suggestion?"

Anu spoke out, while relishing on the delicious lunch prepared by her mom.

"Hand me over the salad, Rinky, will you?" Mrs. Khanna insisted and then she continued, "Well, why don't you call up your friend, Rishav? He is working with the government intelligence department, right? Maybe he is involved in this case and maybe help you to "intrude" as you prefer to term it."

"Oh Mom! You always have an unusual way of saying "Yes". So now I don't have a second through but to prepare myself to "intrude" as I term it." Rinky hugged her mom and they both giggled in laughter.

"I know dear, you are eager to indulge yourself in the case. And who knows it better than your mother. And about relying on Anu, you don't need to. Anyways everyone will be in your suspect list. So go on and solve it baby. Who knows, it may lead to a turning point in your career. And remember Archana Gokhale was an imminent artist, solving her case will surely ring the bells." There was a twinkle in Mrs. Khanna's eyes.

"Ok Mommie dear, let me call up Rishav now and check out."

Rinky took up her mobile phone and returned back to her study. She dialed up Rishav's number.

"Hey Rinky, what's up" Rishav answered.

"Where are you, Rishav? Need to talk and its bit urgent."

"At home. What is it? Any emergency at home."

"Nope. It's about a case I got into today. Need your help, Rishav."

"Aww. Ms Holmes in action, I see. We can meet for coffee, what do you say and talk."

Rinky smiled, "I like that. I know I can rely on you, except your teasing habit."

"Haha. So it's 2:30 PM right now. We can meet at 4 at Roland's Café. Will be near to both yours and my house and the place is perfect to discuss your spooky or thrilling case. Agreed?"

"It's not a spooky case, come on Rishav. Yes, done deal for me. Let's meet at 4 then."

Rinky hung up the phone. She informed her mother about the meet with Rishav and went on to change her dress. Then she sat down and heard the recording of the conversation between her and Anu. She noted down the key points of the conversation in her regular notebook and placed some sticky notes on her whiteboard at the study.

Next she took her head gear and started off towards Roland's café in her scooty.

It was 3:50 PM when she reached the café. She parked her scooty, went inside the café, booked a table for two and sat down waiting for Rishav to arrive.

Rishav arrived around 4:05 PM.

"As usual I am late, and you are before time. I spotted your scooty parked outside and knew Ma'am Rinky is already in."

"And that's why I am a detective and you are not." Rinky spurted out and laughed.

"Ok Ok accepted. Shall we order some coffee and talk."

"Yes, sure. My usual black coffee and cappuccino for you?"

"Yup."

They called up the waiter, placed the order and settled down to talk.

"So, what's your case Rinky? And how can I help you?"

"It's bit sensitive one, Rishav. About the recent suicide by Archana Gokhale. I need your help to investigate the suicide."

"Say again. Are you nuts? It's a government case and its closed. I was myself with the lead detective Mr. Surya Kumar and the decision has already been taken and declared to the public. And out of all the world, why do you want to investigate the case. Did anyone approach you specifically for it?" Rishav was stunned and curious both.

"I know Rishav, the case is closed. And that is why I seek your help. I just guessed your involvement in the investigation and so approached you. I know I can rely on you. Well, you are right, someone approached me stating that she can never commit suicide. But I will not be able to reveal the identity of the person since its risky. The person has confided on me and I need to respect that."

"You have put me into a deep concern, Ma'am. The only way to sneak into it is, you acting as my friend and visiting the premises to scan through the area. Speaking to the people who are close to her can be arranged informally, the documents I have access to can also be checked secretly. But no one on earth should have the slightest hint that you are investigating the case. Rinky, just a doubt. Is the person reliable who requested you to check out the case?"

"No one is reliable Rishav in an investigation. Every single person will be in my radar and in my suspect list. Even then, the person took the trouble to meet me and begged for finding out the reason behind Archana Gokhale's death. So, definitely there is some twist. I may be wrong, but my inner conscience says something is fishy out there. Can you help me please Rishav?"

"Ok as you say, Rinky. But we must be very cautious. As a starting point, let's go to my house and look through some of the documents I have in my laptop. You may gather some preliminary idea of her accounts, diaries she maintained, her contacts, her engagements etc. Tomorrow, I will slip you through Archana Gokhale's house and you can inspect the area. I am officially stationed to visit the place on Monday, doubts hence will be eliminated."

They finished their coffee, served in the midst of their conversation and started off to Rishav's house.

It took about 10 minutes to reach his place, Rinky piggybacking him on her scooty.

"Come over Rinky. Mom has come in for this week, staying with me. She will be delighted to meet you."

"Oh, you never told me. I will be delighted too to meet Aunty. It's been quite a while I had met her. Maybe she can come over to my house and chitchat with my Mom."

"It was a sudden plan, and I was not sure. Anyway, Rinky lets go inside."

They went inside the house.

"Hey Aunty, how are you? So so nice to meet you," Rinky gave a warm hug to Rishav's Mom, Mrs. Joshi.

"Glad to meet you dear. I heard from Rishav that you have started your own practice as a private investigator. So proud of you, Rinky. Keep up the good work and may you shine higher," Mrs. Joshi gave her a peck on her cheek lovingly.

"Sorry Aunty, we will speak in length. But today I have some important discussion with Rishav about one of my cases. Please excuse, but I have told Rishav to drop you at my house. Mom will be happy to see you," Rinky replied with an apologetic tone.

"Sure, don't be sorry at all. Work is first. You both carry on. Meanwhile, I will get you some black tea."

"Mom, keep it small. We just had coffee," Rishav smiled at his Mom.

Both Rinky and Rishav then went inside his study and switched on the laptop.

Secret files of the "Archana Gokhale" case were stored in Rishav's office laptop. He started opening each of them so that Rinky can go through and note down the information essential for the investigation.

In summary, what Rinky jotted down was: Archana Gokhale had returned from a film premiere in Delhi before the day of her death. She was accompanied by the film director and the actors of the film at the premiere. As per the witnesses, she returned to her home at about 8 PM in the evening, alone with only the chauffeur driving the car.

Next morning, the day of her death, she had gone for her normal morning walk and then to the gym. After returning back from the gym, her maid had served the breakfast at about 9 AM at the table. After waiting for about 15 minutes, when she did not arrive at the table, the maid went towards her room to find out. She called up Ms. Gokhale from outside, but there was no response. So, she entered the room, and noticed Ms. Gokhale lying on the bed with her both hands spread out, white foam on her lips, and a small bottle of tablets scattered on the floor. That's when she got terrified and screamed in fear.

The police had come in and had examined the tablets which contained high dosage of Paraquat. There was no signs of strangulation or force on her body in the postmortem report. Neither there was evidence of someone entering her room forcefully. Hence it had become an apparent case of suicide.

"That's the conclusion, Rinky. Her mobile phone was almost crashed on the floor, seems like she tried to get hold of her mobile to call someone but was unable to do so. We were able to retrieve the sim and was able to operate the mobile. I have the contact list that was stored in Archana's phone, which I can print out for you to check."

"That would be great, Rishav. I need to understand who her close contacts were and when and where exactly did she meet them before her death. Also, if she had committed suicide, then definitely she had bought the medicine from any pharmacy. Did you find any pharmacy bill in her room?"

"There's nothing I can recall being discussed by the government sleuths during my visit to Archana Gokhale's apartment. Nor anything reported in the files. But that's a good catch, Rinky. Why don't we check out her room tomorrow to find out?"

"Yes, we will check out. There can be two situations. Either she did not buy the tablets herself, or she did, and the bill is inside her room or tampered; we never know," Rinky's voice sounded serious.

"You are a genius, Rinky. I could never analyze in such a manner. It was an easy conclusion of suicide, but your points do raise questions on the reality."

"I somehow have a feeling that the girl Anu has a point. Anyway, thanks buddy for helping and supporting me with such confidential information at a risk. I hope I can do proper justice to this effort. And oops I blurted out the name of the girl, please that's confidential," Rinky patted Rishav's hand.

"Hey, come on. You can trust me 100% and by the way, I know to whom I am revealing the data. Hope you find out some pivotal evidence tomorrow," Rishav smiled.

"So, when do we meet tomorrow and where?" Rinky questioned as she prepared to leave.

"9 AM should be a good time. I will come over to your house in my car and pick you up. It must look official, so no scooty please Ma'am," suggested Rishav.

"Ok done. I will leave now. Let me scan through the information and the contact list once more today and keep myself prepared for tomorrow's visit."

Rinky wished Goodbye to both Rishav and his mom and returned back to her house.

Before finishing dinner, she narrated all the information collected to her Mom. They both decided to discuss further after her visit to Archana Gokhale's house.

Visit to Ms Gokhale's house

The alarm ticked on at 7 AM.

Rinky switched off the alarm and set about to finish her morning chores.

Both she and Rishav had planned to reach Ms Gokhale's house at around 9 AM. First of all, broad daylight was needed to search for any evidence and proofs. Secondly later in the day, police and other officials from the government departments may visit as the place was yet to be sealed off for further investigation.

Rinky quickly finished her morning tea and breakfast and called up Rishav.

"Hey Rishav, I am ready."

"Great, I will pick you up in next 15 minutes. I am also ready," Rishav answered.

At about 8:30 AM Rishav reached Rinky's house. Archana Gokhale's house was about 30 minutes away and hence they started off without any delay so as not to miss their target of 9 AM.

The house was cordoned off from visitors even though the verdict was declared on Ms. Gokhale's suicide. Rishav displayed his I-card and introduced Rinky to the police constable posted at the house. He had already acquired the necessary permit for her entry, the reason put forward being to perform her research on Archana Gokhale's works as an actress and to brush up her investigating knowledge on how a suicide arena looks like.

They entered the house, it was a duplex apartment with a large living area, a dining area, a study and the kitchen at the ground floor. The upper floor had 3 rooms and a terrace. The apartment had Ms. Gokhale's pictures from various movies, and photoshoots adorning the walls. The décor was artistic, and it proclaimed the aesthetic taste of Ms. Gokhale.

"Why on earth such an affluent person with an elegant taste for beauty, commit suicide?" Rinky thought within herself but did not utter any word on it. She had to be extra careful since the visit was planned not to reveal her intentions.

"Come Rinky, I will show you the bedroom where Ms. Gokhale was found dead," Rishav ushered her into a room biggest among all.

"The maid found her lying on the bed and even when the police came in, they stated the same," Rishav continued.

"I need to check her wardrobe, study table and the other cabinets too. You keep a watch, Rishav. If you notice someone, just nudge me and I will act normal."

"Ok Ma'am. Gotcha," Rishav winked and positioned himself near the door.

Rinky put on her hand gloves and started with the bedside table. It had a small cabinet below. She pulled it out and searched through it. There were some prescriptions and on shuffling them across, she understood Ms. Gokhale had high blood pressure and was under medication. She took a photo with her mobile to check on the Doctor who had prescribed the medicines. There were few tiny bottles of perfume, not of any specific brand. They appeared to be home made and gifted by someone to her as tokens. Rinky also noticed few sleeping pills inside a small medicine box, which indicated she must be having insomnia and took medicines for it. But that can be confirmed only by the doctor who was attending her.

Next, she scanned through Ms. Gokhale's wardrobe. She lifted the piles of dresses slowly to find out any papers or hidden objects but could not find any. She noticed a hidden locker, but it was empty and was not locked too.

"Hey Rishav, was there anything inside the locker?"

"Yes, there was. Many gold and diamond jewelry, all in police custody right now. Once the right custodian is identified and authorized, they will hand it over to that person," Rishav answered.

Rinky sighed and turned back again to check for more clues inside the wardrobe and suddenly noticed a beautiful box tucked away at the back. Carefully, she pulled it out and placed it on the study table. There were letters and greeting cards inside the box, all addressed as "My Love" without any name and from "Yours only" again without any name. It was the same handwriting and same pattern in all of them.

"So, she had a steady boyfriend it seems and she intended to keep it a secret looks like, the way she had preserved each of the letters and cards and tucked them away into a place which is not easily noticeable," Rinky said, her eyes full of curiosity.

"That's a good discovery. And all the more suspicious, how come who is in such deep love think of leaving the world. Or maybe she was ditched in love," Rishav had doubts.

"Yes, it can be either way," Rinky replied as she took the photos of the letters and cards.

"Can I check the kitchen once? Maybe we can get an idea of her food habits."

Yes, sure Rinky. The kitchen is downstairs, let's go."

The kitchen was elegantly decorated too, Rinky was convinced that Ms. Gokhale indeed had a good taste. Each of the crockeries in the kitchen were selected with great care and even the kitchen cabinets were elaborately architected. It seemed strange to her, how at all a person who has beautified her house in such a manner think of ending her life. Maybe Anu was right, Ms. Gokhale did not commit suicide. But then who would like to kill her? Rinky had lots to analyze and check out, she knew it would be tough being a government case and that too with the verdict out.

Rinky shuffled through the cabinets to find oats, various types of nuts, breakfast dietary cereals, light biscuits and cookies, green tea stacked up in the containers. And it was logical as she was an actress, health and physique had to be taken care of.

Then again, the question that popped up in her mind. If she was conscious of herself and her lifestyle, why would she think of committing suicide. But she preferred not to be biased until she finds out substantial evidence and proofs.

"Rinky, we must leave today. Will try to find out another day for a visit. If we spend too much time, there will be suspicions and we may be totally barred from entering the house."

"Yes, agreed. For today, I am fine. I have gained few clues on how to proceed next. I will work on them and we can then come back again later."

Saying this, they both left the house, thanked the constable at guard and proceeded towards Rishav's car.

"Hey, wait, what is Anu doing here?" Rinky suddenly noticed and patted Rishav to look towards a girl in pink t-shirt and blue jeans standing with her back towards them at the roadside where the apartment ends.

"Do you want to check on her?" Rishav asked.

"Yes, let me approach her slowly. Don't want to caution her, as I am not sure what is she doing here and why is she here."

"Go ahead. I will wait here," Rishav agreed.

With light steps, Rinky went near Anu.

"Is that Anu?"

Anu turned back, almost frightened, "Oh Ma'am, it's you. I just was passing by and thought to catch a glimpse of the house. Still, can't believe Archana Ma'am is not there. But it's a surprise to meet you here. Did you come here to visit the house?"

"Yes, I did", Rinky replied.

"And Ma'am did you manage to go inside? Did the constable there allow you? Did you find some clues Ma'am which can prove that Archana Ma'am did not commit suicide?" Anu looked curious as well as worried.

"Well, Anu, not yet. I need to work on it more. I may need some more information from you, so wait for my call in one or two days. I have some advice for you, it's not recommendable to loiter around a house where a suicide has been committed, and still under police control. And over and above, since you feel it's not suicide, it's better to avoid coming near the house for your safety," Rinky's voice appeared stern and serious.

"I understand Ma'am. I am sorry and wont repeat again. I am leaving." Anu turned and hurriedly left. Rinky kept observing her as she increased her walking pace. After few seconds, she turned back and seeing Rinky still standing and staring at her, she just whizzed away as fast as she could.

Once Anu was out of sight, Rinky returned back near Rishav's car.

"She looked to be frightened, Rishav. There was no convincing reason for her to come back and stand near the house unless she had any other intentions."

"Truly suspicious. Anyway get in the car, I will drop you at your house."

"Can we go by this side of the road, Rishav? I want to be sure that she is gone and not hiding somewhere to just wait for us to leave and then come back again."

"Ok sure, let's go," Rishav agreed and started the car.

He followed the direction where Anu had walked past and drove towards the end of the lane and then scanned through both the directions of the lane along the main road. Rinky checked as far as she could, the roadsides and even the bus stands too.

"She has indeed gone, though it appears strange she vanished so fast," Rinky's voice sounded suspicious.

"But I don't think we can do anything right now. Even if we find her, she might just say that she is going to some place and may even not like following her," Rishav said.

"You are correct, Rishav. Let us go back. Anyway I will be asking Anu to meet me tomorrow or day after, I will try to figure out her whereabouts."

It was almost 12:30 PM when Rinky reached her house.

"Thanks a lot for taking the risk, Rishav. It was helpful."

"Now stop acting formal, Rinky. Even I am now eager to find out what is the truth. My innovative mind needs to work out more to find out ways of entering the house."

Rinky laughed, "Ok, I will call you once I get through more on my analysis."

Wishing each other goodbye, Rinky entered her house.

"Mom, lots to tell you. Let me have my shower and then we can discuss while having lunch."

"Great, me too not able to control my curiosity. Looks you picked up an interesting case and there will be fun. I am waiting," Mrs. Khanna sounded jubilant.

Rinky laughed. She loved this enthusiasm of her Mom and she preferred it to be like the way it is. This will keep her Mom's brain active and preferably she will not be occupied with the grief of losing her partner, Rinky's father.

She pecked the cheeks of her Mom and went for shower.

Amalgamating the Facts

"So, were you able to collect some evidence from Ms. Archana's place?" That was the first question from Rinky's mom as both mother and daughter sat for lunch.

"Yes Mom. Two things struck my attention. One is the prescription from her doctor where she had been recommended certain medicines which includes sleeping pills. And the other one is a box hidden away in her closet where she has carefully stored letters from her lover, surprisingly with no names written on it," Rinky replied munching on her food.

"That's interesting. Do you want to call up the doctor to know about her medical history? But you are not authorized for this case, so how do you plan to handle this?" Mrs. Khanna was curious.

"You are right, Mom. I can't just retrieve the information from the doctor. So would certainly have to find out an alternate way. I have to balance between confidentiality as no one is aware of my involvement in this case and then fetching the data that I need for pursuing the investigation."

"Who is your go-to person now, Rinky?"

"I was thinking of Fatima. While checking the prescription and enquiring on the internet, I found out the doctor belonged to Max Memorial Hospital. And coincidently, Fatima is their permanent doctor. After lunch I will call her and check if she can help me."

Rinky finished her lunch and went back to her study. The first thing she did is call up Fatima.

The phone rang and there was Fatima's voice.

"Hey Rinky, what's up. I am just about to go for a surgery. Is it urgent?"

"Oh, apologies Fatima. I should have messaged you before giving you a ring. It won't take much time. Can we catch up sometime later in the day when you are kinda free? I need some urgent information related to a case I am investigating."

"Sure Rinky. Noted. I am gonna give you a call, as soon as I am done with the surgery. I have a break of about an hour before I start attending other patients."

"Thanks a lot, Fatima." Rinky hang up the phone.

Next thing she did was listing her suspects, though at present she had very less in her list. Anu, Dimple Ahuja, Tony D'Souza, the gym instructor, and she kept Anu's boyfriend Jose Branco low in the list. Her next acts were to speak with Dimple Ahuja and Tony D'Souza and find out the name of the gym instructor and his association with Ms. Gokhale.

She called up Rishav.

"Hey Rishav, are you in office? Is it ok to speak with you for a minute?"

"Hold on Rinky, let me step out of the office. Better to be safe." After few seconds of pause, Rishav again spoke up, "Yes, tell me. What is it?"

"Can you try to arrange a meet with Dimple Ahuja, and Tony D'Souza. I heard from Anu they were close acquaintances of Ms. Gokhale. Maybe, you can say I am kind of thinking of preparing a documentary on Ms. Gokhale's works and hence require information about her and her life."

"Let me try it out. As far as I know, Tony D'Souza is not in town. He left after her suicide and seemed has not returned yet. Dimple Ahuja must be easily accessible so let me call her first," Rishav answered.

"That's strange. Is Tony outstation most of the times or is it now? Do you have any idea, Rishav?"

"No, Rinky. I am afraid I am not aware. But I can try to check."

"Sure, check whatever information you have about him. And meanwhile if you can try for a meet with Dimple, then I can speak with her."

"Yes, let me try out and I will call you back." Rishav hangs up.

Next, Rinky called up "The DreamZone", the gym where Ms. Gokhale was a regular. She acted as if she wanted to join the gym and asked whether there will be an instructor to guide her. The gym had three instructors and the receptionist who had attended Rinky's phone mentioned their names as Raj, Vicky and Reena.

"Ah, now I have three names. There are two ways I can find out who was Archana's instructor. Either Anu provides me with more information, or I need to visit the gym, maybe join the classes and eventually find out the correct person." Confusions kept on circling inside Rinky's mind.

She called up Anu.

"Hello Ma'am," answered Anu.

"Anu, can we meet at some café tomorrow?"

"Sure Ma'am. Only that I have been inducted into a new job and my shift ends at 5 PM. Can we meet after that?" Anu asked.

"Not a problem. I will text you the café address and you can come down there. Most probably I will be in by 6 PM, but I will let you know if there is any change." Rinky hung up the phone.

It was very crucial for her to extract as much as information from Anu, since she had been regularly visiting her house and must have noticed many people, their behavioral characteristics, their visits, and their relationship with Ms. Gokhale. The one part which was tough to execute was speaking with her parents. They must be in a trauma after their daughter's death, but at least they will provide correct details about her recent mental well-being, whether she was facing any trouble or was doing good. Rinky has to try but maybe at the end after speaking to all the others.

At about 5 PM, Rinky's phone rang. It was Fatima.

"Hey Rinky, tell me. You wanted to talk. But before that how is your new venture going on?"

"It's pacing up steadily Fatima. Well, I am trying to do some documentary and research work too, and that's the reason why I called you up."

"Oh, wow, that's cool. Interesting one. Sure, tell me how I can help you," Fatima's voice sounded ecstatic.

"You must have recently heard about the death of Ms. Archana Gokhale. I am trying to do some research on her life and her creative works. I felt somewhat strange how come a person with such a fame commit a suicide, so just curious to know more about her. I heard she used to visit a doctor by the name Neeraj Sinha, a cardiologist I suppose. Do you know him by any chance?" Rinky asked.

"Yes, I know him for sure. Renowned cardiologist Dr. Neeraj Sinha, who is a visiting specialist in our hospital. Do you want to meet him, Rinky?"

"Yes Fatima, if you can help arrange that. I will need some 15 minutes not more than that, just to know about her medical history, and whether she was keeping well recently."

"Rinky, well upfront I can tell you. Medical history is a confidential information, which you may not be able to retrieve."

"I know Fatima. I won't ask him straight about medical history, but you know," Rinky gave a pause.

"Ah! Ok I got it. After all you are a detective and a private investigator by profession. You know the trick to ask questions but without breaking the norms," Fatima laughed.

Rinky laughed too, "Yes trust me. Please try Fatima and I definitely owe a dinner with you."

"Oh, come on, Rinky. Now do not be so formal. I will speak to him personally and fix an appointment with you. I don't mind a girly dinner date though."

They both giggled and hang up the phone.

A renowned doctor killed a renowned film actress, is that possible? Rinky stared at her whiteboard and thought explicitly. Doesn't seem to gel well with her calculations. Yet, somehow, she could not leave him out of her suspects and hence wrote down his name in one of the sticky notepad pages and stuck it at the far end of the whiteboard.

Next 1 hour, Rinky spent searching about the two acquaintances of Ms. Gokhale - Dimple Ahuja, and Tony D'Souza. Dimple was a fashion designer and there were several photographs of her in the social media with Ms. Gokhale. It seemed both had a great relation, had traveled many places together, and even attended several events together. In few of the fashion shows organized by Dimple, Ms. Gokhale had been one of the models.

Was Archana a lesbian? Did she have any special relation with Dimple? Is Dimple the "love" mentioned in her letters? Maybe Dimple dumped her, and she decided to kill herself or is it the opposite, she dumped Dimple and hence was killed. Several questions popped up in Rinky's mind as she listed Dimple in her main suspect list.

Rinky could not extract much information about Tony D'Souza, he being less active in social media. From whatever data was available, she could only understand his profession. Tony owned a firm specializing in photography, videography and editing. Her target was to gather more information about Tony and how much he frequented Archana's house or how close was he with her.

She glanced at her watch; it was 9 PM. Neither Rishav nor Fatima called up or messaged, hence it was obvious that none of them had yet managed to do what Rinky had requested. She thought of calling them first thing in the morning.

Before she logged off for the day, Rinky checked out some of the cafes near to Ms. Gokhale's house. There was one called "Chill Out" and looked to be pretty decent. She texted the Google map to Anu and confirmed their meet tomorrow at 6 PM.

At dinner, Rinky discussed her analysis, conversations, and her meetings tomorrow with her mother.

"But Rinky, why are you not asking Anu to come over to our house?" Mrs. Khanna was curious.

"Well, Mom. She is one of my suspects. I found her strangely loitering around Archana's house, when it was not needed. I go out most of the times and you stay alone with the maids. Why to risk inviting her into our house? Not yet sure what her intentions are, unless I am sure her name cannot be eliminated from the list," Rinky answered.

"Got it, dear," Mrs. Khanna smiled.

"Your daughter is intelligent, what do you say?" Rinky smiled too.

"Anyone has any doubt about that? Just tell me the name?"

Rinky laughed heartily at her mom's words.

She finished her dinner, wished her mom "Goodbye" and retired for sleep.

As she closed her eyes, she murmured within herself, "I somehow have a feeling that tomorrow will be interesting."

The Interrogations

Rinky woke up at about 7 AM in the morning, had her cup of tea, and completed her morning chores.

She had a series of actions to complete and had them listed down as she could not afford to miss out any of them. Each phone call and meet were important for her investigation.

At about 8:30 AM, she called up Rishav to enquire whether he was able to arrange for a meet with Dimple and check out on Tony's whereabouts.

"Well Rinky, Tony is still unreachable. I tried many times to call from my mobile. About Dimple, yes she somehow agreed to meet you but did not confirm the date and time. I will call and try to convince her again," was Rishav's reply.

"It's strange that Tony just vanished without anyone being aware of his whereabouts. Or maybe Dimple knows about it. By the way, how have you introduced me to Dimple? I need to be cautious so that we both speak the same and do not contradict each other," Rinky said.

"I told you are conducting a research on Ms. Gokhale and need details about her works and way of working. We have to act accordingly, a slight indication may topple the entire effort of yours."

"Yes Rishav, all are in my suspects list. So, cannot afford to induce any mistakes now. My target is to now extract as much as information possible and the motive behind her death."

Rishav promised to call her back after speaking with Dimple.

Next, Rinky called up Fatima.

"Hey Rinky, I am sorry. I am yet to fix the appointment with Dr. Sinha. He is busy throughout the day today attending several patients and surgeries. But one good thing is, he is comparatively free tomorrow. So, I wanted to confirm the time and call you."

"Understand Fatima, no worries. Please text me once you receive the confirmation."

Rinky hung up the phone. She had no other choice now, but to wait for both Rishav and Fatima's confirmation.

It was 10:30 AM and she had ample time before meeting Anu at 6 PM. She decided to check out the gym 'The DreamZone' and get herself registered. She had very less expectation that Anu would be able to provide the instructor details. She may either hide or may not even be aware. Dimple may also know but there are chances she may not want to reveal all information about Ms. Archana.

She decided to leave, when her phone rang. It was Fatima on the other end.

"Hey Rinky, luckily I managed to secure some time from Dr. Sinha. If you can hold, I can conference him and you can speak for few minutes if that's fine."

"Yes yes absolutely. Conference him," Rinky agreed and was super delighted too.

Fatima conferenced Dr. Sinha and after the initial introduction, Rinky put forward her question to him.

"Sir, I know patient's medical records are confidential. But I just wanted to know whether she had been in depression or suffering from any severe ailment, the reason being a strange curiosity of how a celebrity like her think of committing suicide," Rinky questioned.

"I don't recollect any such illnesses. Insomnia was a botheration for her. And I prescribed medicines. I can only say, she was not very vocal about herself or her ailments. Even if I asked, she avoided and focused her discussion only on her sleep issues," replied Dr. Sinha.

"Understand, thanks a lot Sir. Your information had been extremely helpful. Thank you for agreeing to spend some time for me. Grateful," Rinky said.

"No problem at all, my pleasure."

After finishing off the call, Rinky geared up to visit the gym.

"Mom, I am leaving for few hours. Let me check at the gym whether they can admit me for just a month, will state some temporary stay reason etc." Rinky started preparing herself to leave the house.

"Ok dear, best of luck."

Rinky took her scooty and reached the gym. The receptionist was a lady in her mid 30s and had a jovial face.

"Hi, my name is Rinky. I had called up yesterday to enquire about registration in your gym and who are the instructors who can guide me. But I am just a temporary resident here, putting up at my relative's place. Can I register for say 1 or 2 months," Rinky enquired fluently.

"Yes sure, Maam. Our charges are monthly only. But if you go for yearly subscription then we offer discounts."

"Oh cool, that's great. Then please enroll me for 1 month and then I can decide later. By the way, will I be assigned an instructor or I have to select based on my preferred timing?" Rinky was curious and she had her obvious intentions.

"Maam, all the instructors remain at the gym from 10 AM to 6 PM every day. They are specialized in different gym workouts and hence you can either select with whom to train or you may seek their suggestions. So Maam, if you have decided to enroll yourself, then kindly fill up this form," saying so the receptionist handed over a green colored form to Rinky to fill in her details and signature.

Rinky quickly filled up the form and handed it over to her.

"Can I go inside and check the workout area? I also wanted to speak with the instructors please."

"The monthly charges are Rs. 1500 Maam. If you can pay, then I will provide you the locker keys and access to the gym. Also, I will share the norms and rules of using the gym instruments, the timing, and the dress code. And one more, I would need a passport-size photograph of yours for your id please which you can bring in tomorrow," the receptionist smiled at Rinky.

Rinky understood the receptionist won't let her in unless she clears all the formalities. So she quickly used her Google Pay to clear the monthly charges. The receptionist handed over the locker keys and issued temporary card and access to go inside the gym. Rinky was relieved and she stepped inside the workout area.

The workout area was massive with several people engaged in their daily gym exercises. She noted one lady and one guy assisting and helping others, seemed to be the instructors. First she approached the lady, and introduced herself; guessing it must be Ms. Reena.

"Hi, greetings. My name is Rinky and I have joined new today. Are you Ms. Reena, one of the gym instructors?"

"Hi, yes I am. Welcome to 'The DreamZone'. We have two more instructors, here is Raj." She summoned the guy Rinky had observed before. Rinky shook hands with both of them.

"Is there one more instructor too?" Rinky sounded curious but she somehow controlled herself.

"Oh yes, we have Vicky also as one of the instructors. Poor chap has been in trauma after the death of Ms. Archana Gokhale. She was his special student and her relatives had been mentally torturing him for few days after her death, accusing him of stressing her too hard with workouts and even when she was under a mental distress. He went on a leave after that and had just returned back from his hometown, trying to gear up again."

"Oh I am very sorry to hear that," just the information Rinky had been looking for.

Soon after that, Vicky came out from a room adjacent to the workout and it seemed he had just changed to his gym attire and was prepared to start with his job.

Rinky went forward and introduced herself, "Hi I am Rinky and a new joiner. Would be glad to seek advice from you, Raj Sir and Reena Maam on the daily workouts and exercises."

Vicky turned out to face Rinky. He had a stout and well-built figure, bearded face, 5'8" in height and quite fair complexion. Rinky felt somehow his appearance did not fit in as an instructor. He seemed to be a handsome hunk into some corporate job or business. But yes looks can be deceptive, Rinky assured herself.

"Hi I am Vicky, glad to meet you Rinky and welcome to the gym," there was huskiness in Vicky's voice which was captivating and seductive. Rinky was completely taken by surprise at the sound of his voice. No doubt Ms. Gokhale preferred him as her special instructor, she giggled within herself.

"By the way, if you don't mind, I know this not the appropriate moment. But I heard you were the special instructor of Ms. Gokhale. I am doing some research work on her and would be glad if you could share some of your experiences with her. I know you must have been troubled by her relatives, but as you know the case is now closed by police so hopefully there must be no trouble further onwards," Rinky uttered out as normal she could.

Vicky closed his eyes for a moment, re-opened and facing towards Rinky replied, "Ok no problem. Yes, she was my student. And it is a terrible and tragic death. Never guessed she would commit suicide, being so rich, popular, and full of energy. Though her family members complained of distress and anxiety, I never felt that. Anyway, all now is past. So yes, let me know, if I can I will share information as far as I know which can help your research."

Rinky's job has been accomplished. She thanked all the three instructors after few minutes of chit-chat on what all workouts she must concentrate on and then left for the day.

As she started back towards her home, she knew she had now a good lead to collect more information about Ms. Gokhale. Being a celebrity and an attractive lady, she would definitely share some secrets, passions, interests etc. with Vicky and that's exactly what Rinky wanted to know about.

After returning home, she took her bath, had her lunch and rested for a while. As she expected, the day had already turned to be interesting. Her next meeting was with Anu.

Almost 5 minutes before 6PM, she reached the café "Chill Out", booked a table for two and started waiting for Anu. At around 6:05 PM, Anu came in.

"So Anu, how is your new job?"

"It's good Maam, but missing my old job and Archana Maam," there was sadness and trembling in her voice.

"Are you fine, Anu? You seem to be nervous," Rinky was inquisitive.

"I am trying to be Maam, every moment. The incident had been so tragic, tough for me to overcome and recover from it," there was tears in Anu's eyes.

"I understand. Let's order some coffee and talk."

Rinky ordered cappuccino for Anu and black coffee for herself.

"But tell me one thing honestly, Anu. What were you doing that day in front of Ms. Gokhale's house? You know the place is now sealed and there is police guard. If they find you just loitering in front of the house, they may be suspicious, and you may land up into trouble."

"I am sorry, Maam. I won't repeat that again. I am still not able to believe how come a person who had all what she wanted in terms of fame, and money suddenly commit suicide. She was always so lively and jovial, even when she was upset, she used to smile and have fun with us. I still remember her advising me to enjoy life to the fullest without allowing anxiety and stress to overcome our mind and heart. How come such a person kill herself, without the slightest hint that she was upset. Something is wrong somewhere and that thought is constantly disturbing me. Maam, I know you have visited her house. Were you able to find out anything?"

"Not yet, Anu. I need some information about Dimple Ahuja, and Tony D'Souza. How were their relations with Ms. Gokhale? And if you can try to get hold of Tony as he appears to be out of town and his phone is not reachable most of the times," Rinky put forward her questions.

"Dimple Maam was a close friend of Archana Maam. I feel they both knew each other's secrets. Many times, they used to shut the door of Archana Mam's office room and speak for hours. Expecting that to be work related discussions, we never disturbed them or even knock the door. In fact, we were almost forbidden to do so. Though I had once gained all my courage and asked her about the meetings as sometimes those were prolonged, and meals were skipped. But I never received a satisfactory answer and hence did not dare to repeat my questions. Also, she was my employer and I had to respect her privacy," Anu explained.

"And what about Tony?" Rinky's second question.

"Tony Sir was professionally related to Archana Maam. He had accompanied her in many visits. Their discussions, however, were not hush hush, but happened openly in front of us. In fact, I was present always preparing the notes, meetings, visits etc. Not sure the reason behind his disappearance though."

"Can you do one thing, Anu? Try reaching Tony in these few days. If you are able to, share your sadness and grief with him and try to find out why he has vanished. Assure him that he can confide to you safely and if he still doesn't yield then we have to consider the matter seriously. Can you?"

"Yes Maam, I will try my best and inform you," Anu agreed.

Meanwhile coffee had been served. They both finished the coffee, Rinky cleared the bill and they both bid goodbye to each other and left for their destinations back home.

The Unknown Tales

Rinky stared at the board where she had pinned down the names of the suspects in small chits of paper.

Who can it be? She thought.

It can be Anu herself, trying to save herself from the crime or maybe trying to prove someone guilty for revenge. She has a boyfriend but did not speak much about him. But his chances of being guilty are less as he was not very frequent to the city and to Ms. Gokhale's house. Maybe Ms. Gokhale committed suicide, but then again why. Being so established and popular, earning tons of money; why would she think of such an action unless she was gripped with any unavoidable circumstances.

Next are her two acquaintances – Dimple and Tony. Do they have any purpose of murdering her? And if yes what would that be? They do not have any blood relations, so the thought of acquiring her property and wealth is out of question unless they had plans of betraying her or fooling her in some way. Or maybe they both are not guilty at all and may not be aware of her enemies. It is important for her to find out what do they know about Ms. Gokhale, eventually may help her to find out some clues to her investigation.

The Doctor part also did not work well. Seemed she never had any severe medical issues. She only took sleeping pills which again increases the chances of suicide.

Rinky was completely engrossed in her thoughts when her phone rang. She collected herself and checked the caller. It was Rishav.

"Yes Rishav, tell me".

"Good news, Rinky. Dimple agreed to meet us tomorrow at around 10 AM. It had to be in the morning as she had to start for her job at around 11 AM. So we have 1 hour to speak with her."

"That's great, Rishav. I will manage in 1 hour. We need to harp on her emotions a bit else she may not speak her heart out."

"Yes, I understand what you are hinting at. I have mentioned about the café near to Ms. Gokhale's house, "The Zulu". Let's meet up there."

"Ok Rishav, I will reach before 11 AM. Can't afford to lose any minute."

Next day, Rinky was at the planned destination at 10:45 AM. Rishav also reached after 5 minutes. They booked a table for three at the café and waited for Dimple.

Dimple arrived at around 11:05 AM and as she approached them, Rinky observed her carefully. She was slim, tall, and beautiful; can easily flaunt herself as a model or an actress. Her physical appearance matched with her Facebook profile. For a fashion designer, it is appropriate to keep one's physique perfect and wear her own creations; and Dimple exactly seem to fit in that description.

"Thank you, Ms. Dimple Ahuja, for agreeing to meet me. I am Rinky," Rinky extended her to greet me.

"My pleasure, Ms. Rinky," Dimple acknowledged her greetings. She shook hands with Rishav as well and pulled a chair to sit down.

"Ms. Ahuja, you must be quite disturbed by your friend's sudden demise. First of all, please accept my condolences. Somehow, I have deep regards for Ms. Gokhale as an artist. Her works are amazing, and it is a great loss to the film industry. As my respect to her and being her fan, I want to publish a research article on her works and her professional life. You are the best person whom I can speak to and hence requested Rishav to fix an appointment with you. I am sorry if I have bothered you, but I won't take much time of yours," Rinky spoke carefully and cautiously.

"Please don't be sorry. I am still unable to accept the fact that she is no more. We were besties. There was not a single day when we did not speak and sometimes for hours. She was so ambitious, wanted to produce and direct films and attain worldwide fame. It is difficult for me to digest that she committed suicide. But fact is fact and have to embrace that, even though it is bitter," Dimple's eyes were watery.

Rinky felt her sorrow which did not seem to be fake.

For the next 30 minutes, she put forward many questions and listened to Ms. Dimple attentively.

Among the various information shared, she could understand Ms. Gokhale was a travel freak and loved beaches. She loved to spend her time in the Maldives, Mauritius, Bali, Goa, Thailand, and Australia. In fact, she was a frequent traveler to these places and stayed in the same hotels; almost well-known among the hotel staff.

She never dreamt of a family life as she was too ambitious in her career yet a fun-loving party-goer. But then in between her conversations, Dimple mentioned about Ms. Gokhale being entangled into some love affair unknowingly which troubled her a lot until she successfully freed herself. But she did not dwell into the details, quickly drifted away from the topic.

"Well, I am sorry. Please do not write about this in any of your articles. I do not want her personal life to be known to anyone. Can you promise?"

"Absolutely, Ms. Dimple. That's a promise. Even I respect her privacy and wont mention a word about it. You can trust me."

"Thanks a lot," Dimple's eyes were full of gratitude.

At about 12:10 PM, Dimple excused herself and left.

"Love and respect for Ms. Gokhale is clearly visible in her eyes. I cannot find any good reason why she can ever think of a murder. The one thing now concerns me is the troubled love affair of Ms. Gokhale. I need to dig into this more," Rinky spoke after Dimple left.

"But how, Rinky. Except Dimple, I doubt anyone can help us with that information. Ms. Gokhale's facebook page also doesn't give any hint."

"Come on, Rishav. She was troubled with that affair, why on earth she will flash about the relation in public. Dimple mentioned about the places which were frequented by Ms. Gokhale during her travel journeys. Normally, travel freaks meet different kinds of people and love to socialize. It maybe she met that person in any of her trips. But then to find out whether she lived in with that person or even spent a vacation together, we need to trace the hotels in these destinations."

"And that's quite a humongous task with the case being closed," Rishav uttered out.

"Rishav, now I want to find out the truth. Even if Anu backs out, I want to see this to the end," there was sudden determination in Rinky's voice.

That same look and same voice – Rishav immediately knew she cannot be deterred now from her objective. During her days at the news agency, while she was working at their investigation department, the moment she immersed into a case and started discovering the clues; Rinky's face had the same look and the same voice.

"I know, Maam. Nothing can stop you now. Let me check out on some of the informers I have in Goa, and Thailand. The other places will be tough with the complicacies of international borders, but I will try my best," Rishav replied.

"Thanks a lot".

"At your service, Maam". And they both laughed.

Rishav indeed checked out with his informers at Goa and Thailand for the next two to three days and tracked down two hotels – "Majestic Glow" at Thailand and "Sonam Bay" at Goa. But surprisingly none were 5-star or 7-star hotels but had a beachfront and located at a secluded place.

"Rishav, I think Ms. Gokhale wanted to spend her vacation in peace and in solitude. That must be the reason she selected these two hotels. You were mentioning about someone accompanying her right?" Rinky questioned.

"Yes, but that was only in Thailand, with some guy named Joel Gonsalves. At Goa, she had booked for self only," answered Rishav.

"Oh, that's strange. Was Joel her ex and was he a resident of Thailand? Or maybe he was just a temporary accomplice. Were you able to find out any details about this Joel guy?"

"Not really, Rinky. Only that it seems he owned some business, maybe a hotelier but not confirmed yet. Have to dig into it more."

"Hmm. Can we by any chance find out the hotels she had stayed in the other destinations?" Rinky was curious.

"Chances are feeble. But let me try. May need 3 or 4 days more," Rishav replied.

"That should be fine. Meanwhile, let me try to speak with Vicky, the gym instructor of Ms. Gokhale and find out some information of use and relevance."

Rinky had started attending the gym but somehow during the first two days she could not find Vicky, seemed he was busy with some alternate assignments. Luckily on the third day, she met him and did not want to waste her chances.

"Where you on vacation? I came here for last two days but could not attend your classes," Rinky placed her question cautiously trying to hide her curiosity as much as possible.

"No, I was busy with a client whom I have been assigned to recently," answered Vicky in short.

"Wow, you are lucky to be working with renowned celebrities," Rinky smiled as she continued to work out following Vicky's instructions.

There was no answer from Vicky though.

Rinky continued after a pause, "Was it an exciting experience to work with Ms. Gokhale? She must have been fitness freak."

Vicky turned at her, "Is there any specific reason of asking about Ms. Gokhale? You know that she is dead right."

"Sorry, but if you remember I had mentioned that I am doing some research on her works and professional life. So was just curious," Rinky replied hesitatingly.

"Aw ok. It had slipped my mind, too much work pressure."

"Yes indeed, I understand. So, like how was she? Was she regular in the gym?" Rinky carried on.

"She was regular and punctual. And yes, kind of fitness freak, overtly ambitious and adamant," there was a heavy sigh in Vicky's voice. He turned himself away, picked up his towel and water bottle, slowly walked towards the glass window and stared outside.

"I see," Rinky's eyes did not miss the depressed expression visible on Vicky's face.

After few seconds, he returned back and requested to carry on with the workouts. Meanwhile, other members had arrived and so Rinky controlled her inquisitiveness for a while. Though her mind was not inclined to continue with the exercises, yet she kept her cool and pretended to be normal.

The moment the session was over, she almost rattled out her questions.

"Was she very particular about her diet? Did you prescribe her some routine? Was it only food or additional intakes like some nutrient bars etc.?"

"Hold on, Ma'am. You are too fast," Vicky stared at Rinky surprisingly, "Well yes I had a diet prescribed to her. She diligently followed it."

"Was it only normal cooked food, fruits, vegetables or she required additional intakes?" Rinky questioned again.

"Is this topic important for your research?" Vicky wondered.

"It may seem unimportant for a normal individual like you and me. But you know for celebrities like Ms. Gokhale its vital. People want to know about her food habits, gym habits etc. and intend to pursue them sometimes. These points will be definitely crucial for my article. I will be grateful if you can share, please," Rinky almost pleaded.

"Ok then. Apart from normal food, yes, I had to suggest additional intakes like protein, vitamin, iron etc. to maintain balance of nutrients in her body. Though she did not follow my instructions once," Vicky's voice sounded low.

"Why, what happened?"

"What happened? Oh no, nothing significant. It's like she was stressed out of work and then the workouts, so I suggested. But she did not follow and was not well for a while. Just flashed my mind so," Vicky returned back to his normal tone.

Nothing went unnoticed with Rinky.

Something seems to be fishy and wrong. Rinky's inner conscience hinted her. She knew she had to find out more questions to probe Vicky. Maybe he had a soft corner for her or vice versa or maybe it was mutual. She had to find out what else he knew about Ms. Gokhale. If Vicky vanishes some day, then it will be tough for her. So, she decided to visit the gym regularly for the next few days.

Life of a Celebrity

"The dots are not reconciling Mom," Rinky's voice sounded restless as she sat at the breakfast table with her mother.

"They will, dear. Maybe you are missing something or maybe you need to probe more on the available information and Archana's acquaintances," Mrs Khanna assured her.

"Oh, you are a darling, Mom. I think I should get back to Ms. Gokhale's house. I only went there for one day and I am 100% sure I have not captured all the clues. Let me check with Rishav immediately," Rinky started dialing his number on her mobile.

"No wait, Rinky. First finish your breakfast. Remember an empty stomach idles the brain. So be calm, finish your food and then call Rishav".

Rinky smiled and nodded her head in agreement. She finished her breakfast, went to her study, and dialed up Rishav.

"Yes Maam. Good morning. Tell me what can I do for you. Any new conclusions?"

"Rishav, you need to again arrange for a visit again to Ms. Gokhale's house. I feel we have missed capturing some crucial evidence. We need to perform a thorough search in every nook and corner of her house. Can we somewhat do it today?"

"Let me check out the constable who is in guard today at Ms. Gokhale's house. Give me some 15 mins and I will call you back."

"Ok Rishav, will wait."

Rinky utilized the 15 minutes noting down the tasks she needed to perform. One was to connect with Tony and she sincerely hoped Anu can help. Next, she also had to understand the relation between Anu and Ms. Gokhale and the only person who can provide the information is Dimple. But then how can she enquire about Anu without hinting about her intentions. Somehow, she has to gain Dimple's confidence.

Third will be to continue probing Vicky so that he reveals some crucial information. Maybe focus on his emotions. Somehow Rinky felt he had special fascination for Ms. Gokhale. Last was to find out about the mystery man Joel, maybe Archana's ex-lover.

Rinky was completely engrossed in her thoughts, when her mobile rang and it was Rishav.

"Good news. Today the constable is different from the one who was there before when we went to Ms. Gokhale's house. So, I can again play on the same excuse as the person now at guard doesn't know you. If you are fine, I can pick you up in about 30 minutes and we can visit the house."

"That's simply great. Absolutely, 30 mins is fine. The earlier it is, the better."

Rinky put on a casual shirt and jeans and in the next 30 minutes was out with Rishav in his car, towards Ms. Archana Gokhale's house.

Rishav introduced Rinky as a senior police investigator researching on the reasons behind her suicide, to the constable at guard.

They went inside her study and bedroom and started critically searching the desk and cupboard drawers for any hidden evidence. But there were no such noticeable clues to be traced.

"What next?" asked Rishav.

Rinky sighed for few seconds and then moved towards Archana's wardrobe. She started scanning in between her clothes and suddenly felt a hard wooden object. She pressed it and surprisingly noticed a small hidden closet inside the wardrobe.

"Come here, Rishav. Looks to be a secret chamber."

"That's a great discovery. Let's check out what is inside it."

There was a file inside the chamber which did not seem to be very old. They pulled it out and placed it on the table nearby to search the content.

"This is a prescription from a gynecologist. Check it, Rishav, Archana Gokhale was pregnant".

"Oh No. She had kept it secret".

"And it's not very old, one year back. Is that the trouble she had faced with her ex-lover? Seems to be connected to what Dimple had referred to."

They found the blood test reports too which the doctor had prescribed.

Rinky started searching through the rest of the papers and found a second prescription. But it was from a hospital in Maldives.

"Why on earth in Maldives? Isn't it strange?" asked Rishav.

"No Rishav. The calculations are matching. Read the prescription, she went for an abortion. And she did it in Maldives to save her reputation, far away from here where people won't be aware."

"Truly, life of a celebrity is tough. Even though you have money, but then difficult to lead a happy personal life. Always being under the radar of suspicion and scandal and struggling to keep the reputation intact." Rishav ended with a sigh.

"But then, if she had been able to eliminate her problem, why should she commit suicide. And as far as we know, nothing was in the news about her. In fact, the media never reported of any scandal associated with her. There were some about her remarks on certain films and political issues, but those happen with every other celebrity and quite normal in the film industry."

"What are your next plans, Rinky?"

"Need to speak with Tony. I have asked Anu to try and establish a connect with him and convince him for a meet. Let's go Rishav. I think we can carry this evidence. Don't think anyone will ever discover the secret chamber."

"Absolutely. Ok, let's go."

At home, Rinky decided to call Anu before lunch to check whether she had any success in connecting with Tony. But before she could, Anu had dropped a message requesting for a call.

"Yes, Anu. Tell me. Any luck?"

"Yes Maam. I was able to speak with Tony Sir, mentioned your name, and about your research work on Archana Maam as you had instructed."

"So, what did he say?" Rinky was curious.

"He has returned to Mumbai today morning. And that he can meet only at his house. But he told me not to share his address in a message or WhatsApp but to show you the location."

"Oh, interesting. Can we meet sometime in the afternoon? You can tell me which location to come to and then from there you can direct me to his house."

"Sure Maam. Let me check back with him and I will give you a ring."

"Ok Anu, will wait."

Rinky took her bath, and joined her mother for lunch. As usual they started chatting, the topic obviously being the investigation. She discussed about the prescriptions and her upcoming meet with Tony.

"You are progressing well dear. Hope you are not leaving out anyone from your suspicion list?" Mrs Khanna's eyes twinkled.

"You probe me always at the appropriate time. Yes Mom, I am not even leaving out Anu. Decided to gain the confidence of Dimple to extract details about her".

"Excellent, Rinky. Be careful not to eliminate anyone".

"Sure Mom". Though Rinky was convinced on the people she was scrutinizing but her mother's words seemed to carry some message which she was unable to decipher.

Anu called at around 4 PM and informed that Tony was ready to meet at his house where he had an office space too.

They both agreed to meet at Topher Square, which was near to Tony's place, at around 5:30 PM. Anu informed she was not at home and would be little late in reaching the destination.

Rinky reached Topher Square at sharp 5:30 PM but could not locate Anu anywhere nearby. She decided to wait. After 5 minutes, she noticed a girl running towards her from the opposite side of the road and soon she recognized Anu. She could not locate any bus or cab from where Anu could have descended. But located a bike with a man at the driver seat. She tried to focus her attention on the man, though the distance was quite far yet she felt an instinct of familiarity with someone.

"Sorry Maam, I am bit late," Anu reached, almost panting.

"No worries. You had been somewhere?"

"Yes Maam. My boyfriend is in town. So went out for some shopping."

"Is he on the bike?"

"Yes Maam," Anu blushed.

"Oh, wow. You could have asked him to come here. I could have met him."

"He is a bit introvert. Sorry."

"Hey don't be sorry, Anu. That's perfectly fine. Will you guide me to Tony's house?"

"Yes Maam. Please follow me."

Anu started walking along the same side where they met. Rinky again looked at the man on the bike, Anu's boyfriend. She has definitely seen him somewhere, the inquisitiveness registered in her mind.

After a 5 minutes walk, they reached near Tony's house. It was an apartment complex with a heavy gate for the entrance.

"His flat number is CL202. Zone C, Block L, Floor 2 and house number 202. Please state your name at the gate and mention whom you want to meet. They will assist you. Tony Sir has informed the guard."

"Thank you Anu. That was a great help. You go and spend time with your partner."

"My pleasure, Maam. He will be leaving day after tomorrow, so hanging around," Anu smiled, waved Rinky and left.

At the entrance gate, Rinky registered her name and started walking towards Zone C, Block L as guided by the guard.

She took the elevator, reached house number 202, and rang the bell.

Tony opened the door. A tall handsome fan with a medium fair complexion in a casual t-shirt and jeans. Rinky was now certain, Archana Gokhale preferred her close acquaintances to be smart and good looking.

"Ms Rinky Khanna?"

"Yes"

"Please come in. I am Tony D'Souza."

Rinky stepped inside.

The house was fashionable in appearance, with a western décor. Furniture neatly placed, simple yet artistic.

"Please have a seat."

"Sure, thanks."

Rinky sat down on a sofa and took out her notebook, while Tony sat on a couch in front but not face to face.

"You must have heard from Anu about my willingness to publish about the Life of Ms. Archana Gokhale. I am a great fan of hers and this will be a tribute to her and her works."

"Yes, Anu informed. Frankly speaking, her sudden demise is still a mystery. Police concluded suicide, but it is difficult to believe. She had multiple projects in her mind and her ambitions were like enormous. At the peak of her career, why would she at all think of killing herself. Maybe she had something bothering her which none of us knew. Anyway, please tell me what you want to know about her."

"Do you think it may not be suicide? In fact, I am also unable to erase from my mind the suicide fact, though I am just an ordinary fan."

"My thoughts doesn't matter, Ms Rinky. Even I am an ordinary man and she was a celebrity. Let's park those discussions, anyhow police knows better than us."

"Sure," Anu started, "Can you please describe about her professional life and her association with the film world?"

"Archana and I are schoolmates. After we left school, she went to study modeling and I at the film institute. I pursued my studies on films, videos, etc. Since we were not in the same city at that time, me at Mumbai and she at Pune, our connect was not so frequent. Few exchange of messages and some rare phone calls. It was at one of our school reunions, I finally met her. She had then already stepped into the ladder of success and was a known celebrity. We discussed about the projects she had in her plan. I was amazed at her intelligence, ambitions, and thoughts. My perception of actresses was like they are only concerned about their looks, attire, fame etc. but Archana seemed to be different from them. I truly appreciated that and agreed to be part of her venture in creating short films mostly documentaries and biopics."

Tony took a pause.

"It was going on so well. We had so many discussions, visited many places within and outside India. We met so many people, built rapport and connects. Never imagined she would just go away and now all her dreams are gone. None of the projects can complete without her. She was the brain behind all these initiatives."

Rinky can feel the sadness in his voice. It was clear Archana Gokhale had a deep influence on all the people she had been with – Dimple, Anu, the gym instructor and now Tony. Definitely there was something unique and magical in her. If that is so, why would someone want to kill her.

"You mentioned you had been to many places. Where all the places you visited, just curious? Hope you don't mind sharing the names?"

"Yes sure. We had been to Thailand, Mauritius, Maldives, Goa for some luxury shootouts and then to Arunachal Pradesh, Nagaland, Meghalaya where she wanted to film documentaries on the tribal life of India."

Rinky was able to match the dots a bit on the places visited by Ms. Archana.

Was Tony her secret boyfriend? Was the baby from him? But then Dimple mentioned she had a troubled affair, if that is so then why would she continue her connect with Tony?

Several questions splashed across her mind.

As Tony went on describing about their tours and projects, Rinky quickly glanced across the room and observed some photographs framed and kept as display.

"Do you have any photographs with her and her team?"

"Yes, ofcourse. Let me show the one I have kept here". Having said this, Tony stood up and took one of those framed photos and handed over to Rinky.

"This was a trip at Goa," Tony said.

The photo was of a beach party with Archana Gokhale, Tony D'Souza and Dimple Ahuja, and some other people whom she could not recognize.

"It was New Year and we had a blast".

"Seems you all had real fun". Rinky smiled and handed over the photo frame to Tony.

"Did you observe any unusual behavior before her death? Maybe she was disturbed or stressed."

"No, Ms Rinky. She was absolutely normal. As per my experience, only once I had observed unusual behavior or rather, I will say she was disturbed but that too I think one year back. She was less attentive which hampered her ongoing projects for quite some time. Even she went to Maldives suddenly without even informing anyone. She never spoke about her issues though, slowly she returned to her normal state."

Another dot matched. But then if Tony was not her ex-lover then who was it?

"Who were her close friends? Do you have any other reference with whom I can talk to also?"

"Dimple Ahuja was her close buddy. I think they discussed almost everything and every day."

"I see. Did she have any boyfriend? Just curious."

"Celebrities meet different kinds of people. It is tough to understand their personal life. Though I respected her professionally, I was unaware and ignorant of her personal life. She loved traveling and visited many places just for vacation or maybe with someone which I never felt necessary to be aware of."

Rinky felt the answer to be diplomatic. Maybe he knows something and doesn't want to disclose. Or maybe he did not appreciate her personal life.

Rinky glanced at her watch. It was 6:40 PM. She did not want to miss her gym classes.

"Thank you so much for the information. I have to leave now, need to attend another event. It was nice meeting and speaking with you. By the way, Anu was mentioning that you were out of town. Must be another interesting assignment?" Rinky closed her notebook, preparing to leave.

"Oh, no no it was not an assignment. Every year, I visit an ashram of my Guru where we observe detox from the regular daily life. My mobile is switched off on those days. The death of Archana was a big disturbance, and I was finding it difficult to concentrate. So decided to stay away for a while. The burden of projects and her unexpected suicide, I was in a mess. Have to return back to my normal life and find out a way to complete the projects."

"I understand. Time will heal up, I am sure."

"Thank you, Ms Rinky. And do please share the article link after you publish. Will be glad to read it."

"I will, sure". Rinky left Tony's place and hurried for the gym.

Plan Refurbished

It was 7:15 PM when she reached the gym entrance and was almost panting for breath. She had earlier called up the gym and had requested them exclusively to leave a message for Vicky to stay back for a while for few instructions from him. The gym, however, did not promise that it will work out.

With fingers crossed, Rinky entered the gym and to her surprise Vicky was there. And somehow it seemed he himself had arrived late.

"Hi Vicky, thank you for waiting," Rinky was pleased.

"Sorry, thank you for?" Vicky seemed surprised.

"Ah thank you for waiting. I had left a message for you, requesting if you could stay back for a while as I just needed some few instructions that's all."

"Oh no, I am not working. It's that I had some prior commitments and hence had to step out. My bag and other accessories were left in the gym so just came to collect them."

"Ah ok, got it. Never mind. Can I ask you few questions if you don't mind please?"

Vicky looked up, not a reluctant face though, "Yes go ahead, but please keep it short."

"Yes sure absolutely. Did Ms Archana skip her gym classes for a considerable amount of time?"

"What does that have to do with your article?"

Rinky understood the question was a stupid attempt, but she had no other choice as she needed to verify the pregnancy part. She summoned Vicky closer and whispered, "Please understand. I need add some spices to the article else it won't sell so much. I am trying to find out some unusual stuff in her life which I can focus on. Don't worry I am not publishing any name in my article."

"Ok, but I don't remember anything specific incident as such. There were few instances when she did not visit the gym while I was out of town. And there were other instances when she was out of town for her assignments," answered Vicky.

There were few instances when she did not visit the gym while I was out of town.

- The sentence was a bit suprising for Rinky. She thought, "Why was Archana obsessed with Vicky? Why did she stop visiting the gym when Vicky was absent? She can do her own workouts and can even ask other gym instructors to help her? What was so special about Vicky?"

Keeping her curiosity aside, Rinky asked, "Did she suffer from any specific ailment that prevented her from heavy workouts?"

"Hey listen, enough. I am not aware of her personal life in details. If you need spices, go and ask the media. They can shower you with all entertaining info. I was her instructor in gym and that's all," Vicky suddenly was agitated.

Rinky was immediately conscious, she cannot afford to lose anyone's trust now.

"I am sorry, please calm down. My sources are less, and I do not have connects in media. I am just an ordinary human being and a writer. Please bear with me. I promise I won't ask any more questions on her personal life," she pleaded.

"That's ok. Never mind. Sorry I just lost my temper for a while. So you were looking for some instructions."

Rinky knew her day was done. She won't be able to ask any more questions today.

"Yes yes right, I just wanted to verify the postures for few free-hand exercises. And if you can just jot down the breakfast options which you had referred earlier. Here is my notepad and pen."

Rinky handed over the notepad and pen to Vicky, who scribbled down some of the diet option for her. For the next 10 minutes, Vicky demonstrated some of the exercises and then parted for the day. After he was gone, Rinky had in fact no intention to stay back. But then she had to remain normal and hence completed few workouts for the next 30 mins and stepped out for home.

Mrs Khanna was at the living room, sewing a table runner with her crochet. As Rinky entered the door entrance, she spoke without lifting up her head, "Very late today, any significant progress?"

Rinky sighed, dumped her gym kit bag on the floor, and sat down on the sofa.

"No Mom. The only significant part is Archana was pregnant and we know she was single and not a mother. So definitely she had undergone abortion. And none of her acquaintances I spoke with are aware of it. Tony says she once vanished and went to Maldives. The gym instructor Vicky mentioned about her absence from gym when he was out of town. And then Rishav traced out that she used to visit places with someone. The dots are connecting in some instances and in some instances they are not. Is there someone else in this whole plot whom I am missing? I am clueless Mom. Further today I tactfully collected the handwriting of Vicky but it is not matching with the love letters I retrieved from Archana's wardrobe. So it seems Vicky is also ruled out. Only there are two people left – Joel with whom Archana had been to Thailand but seems there is no clue about the whereabouts of the person and other is Anu's boyfriend, which is a mystery at this point as I have not met the person at all."

"Celebrities are usually very conscious of their sexual life and desires. And the stature Archana Gokhale had, it is bit strange that she conceived. Did that not strike you, Rinky?"

"Wow what a hint, Mom. Yes, you are right, she is not a fool to conceive and ruin her reputation. So definitely she must have done this consciously," Rinky's eyes lit up, "But then did she go for abortion, or it happened naturally? Though the prescription says abortion but that doesn't answer my question. I am clueless again," she again sighed and laid back on the sofa.

"Come on, my dear. You are a smart investigator. If you lose hope so fast, then how come you can grant justice to innocent people. You freshen up. Let's have dinner, recharge yourelf, either think again or sleep, wake up tomorrow and think in a cool peaceful state of mind. You will find clues, definitely it's there, either concealed somewhere or its present in front of you, you need to decipher them," Mrs Khanna placed her hands on Rinky's head lovingly and went upstairs for arranging dinner.

Rinky took a shower, and made herself comfortable in her house gown. After dinner, she sat with her mom at the balcony, relaxed.

"Mom, there is one more character Joel. Archana had spent a vacation with him in Thailand, and no other places. Or maybe she had, we do not have the information. Rishav is checking out. This guy is a mystery still. Either he was Archana's secret boyfriend or maybe a temporary one, not sure. He is the only person whom I have not spoken to, in fact, still do not have much details about him."

"Rishav is a smart chap, he will definitely crack out some information. Am sleepy now, you also take some rest and think again tomorrow with a fresh mind."

Mrs Khanna retired to her room for the day. Rinky stayed back at the balcony, unable to stable her mind. She closed her eyes and started visualizing the characters one by one.

Dimple was Archana's bestie, yet she never knew about her pregnancy or she knew and did not share the incident with Rinky. Archana had spoken about her troublesome affair to Dimple which proves they were the best of friends. Definitely the pregnancy has much more story to it. Tony suddenly went for a meditation detox after Archana's death. Was he in love with her secretly? The Maldives part matched from his version and the prescription. The Maldives trip reality can be verified with Dimple, that will prove certainty. Vicky had a soft corner for Archana, that's evident from his conversations. Was he the secret boyfriend? Doesn't seem to be, since a celebrity like her won't fall for a gym instructor. It can hardly be an infatuation and doesn't seem to be linked with the love letters. Anu will not have the audacity to murder a person, she needs to possess exquisite caliber to perform such an act and go scot-free. Moreover, being so confident and approaching Rinky, speaks about her honesty. Or on the contrary, maybe she was forced to visit Rinky. And then comes Joel, a complete unknown character. If Archana had a tendency to engage into temporary relations, then there can be many such Joels. Either Joel was her ex or just an insignificant character. Anu and Joel needed further deep dive; their whereabouts have to traced.

Rinky opened her eyes. She had a clear plan for tomorrow, jotted down in front of her. First, she will have to check with Rishav whether he had been able to collect further information on Joel. And also check whether there were many other Joels she had been with or only one person. Second is to visit Archana's house again to check if there are any old photographs or pen drives etc. Third is to meet Dimple again and probe her on the Maldives trip. If she was so close to Archana, she will know. Fourth will be to request Rishav to check on Anu, and her whereabouts.

Though her plan was set, her inner conscious kept on poking her that she was missing something. Yet she was unable to figure out what was that?

"Maybe Mom is right. I should sleep and rest for today. A fresh mind may come up with more ideas," Rinky said to herself.

She stood up, closed the balcony doors, switched off the lights and walked towards her room. As she passed by her mother's room, she peeped inside, smiled and said to herself, "You are such a big strength Mom. You have lost your partner, my dad. Yet still you are so strong, your rational thinking motivates me to pursue my career. I love when you provide me those small hints to solve my cases. You are super intelligent, and I love you. I will solve this one too, I promise." She blew a flying kiss to her mom and with silent footsteps went to her room.

Hurriedly she noted down her plan for tomorrow in one of her notepads so that none is missed out. Suddenly she felt hopeful for a better tomorrow and smiled again to herself.

She retired to her bed and closed her eyes. Before she could settle down, suddenly a light flashed across her mind and she knew what she had missed. Hurriedly she jotted down in the notepad where she had planned out her schedule for the next day. She smiled and felt glad about herself. A jump into her bed, lights switched off, she was back to her mood. In a minute's time, Rinky was in deep sleep, the tiredness of the day overtook her in entirety.

A Discovery and A Confidant

"**G**ood Morning Rishav, any news for me?" Rishav was the first person whom Rinky called up after her breakfast.

"Good Morning Rinky. Not a very positive news, that's the reason I did not call you up. Was waiting for some info, but seems it is tough. I could extract few photographs where Ms Archana is seen with a guy in Maldives, Goa, and Thailand. But it is hard to guess whether the guy is the same person or different. The photos are printed from CCTV camera recordings hence quite tough. I got them printed for you also, will drop by your house in the afternoon, and sending you the soft copies too. Maybe your detective eyes can decipher any clues, I was not able to dig heads and tails out of it."

"Ok send it over. Let me check out. One more thing, can we visit Archana's house again. I think there are some more secrets to her life," Rinky waited for an answer from Rishav.

"Let me check the guard on duty. In few days' time the police is going to circulate a notice of handing over Ms Archana's property and belongings to any of her acquaintances, else government will take over. So you need to check out thoroughly this time, we may not get a second chance," replied Rishav.

"Got it, looks like this will be the last time," Rinky chuckled.

"Aha, seems the wait is going to be over soon. I can't just keep myself calm to hear the result," Rishav's voice sounded exciting.

"Patience, patience, my dear friend. Few strings are still loose, and I am trying to tighten them a bit. If I succeed, then things will be crystal clear."

"Ok Ok my highness. Let me check out what can I do for you."

"One more request Rishav. Can you check on Anu and her whereabouts. Maybe click some photographs of her with her boyfriend. I am yet to check on that guy, seems a shy person."

"Cool, it will be done. Not a tough job after all," Rishav's voice was positive.

Both hung up the phone in a minute.

Rinky's next call was to Dimple. After a 10 minute conversation, she convinced Dimple to meet her again. Though she suggested a coffee shop but somehow the other party was not eager to discuss about Archana in public. The meeting time was agreed around 4 PM same day.

Meanwhile, Rishav had shared the screenshots, as promised, to Rinky. After concluding her call with Dimple, Rinky opened her WhatsApp to check the images. Being a known face, Ms Archana seemed to be visible, but the guy in each of the images was not facing the camera which made it tough to recognize. She transferred the images to her laptop to zoom out and probe into them.

In 30 minutes of time, there was a knock at the door. Rishav had sent across the hard copy of the images with one of his trusted person. Rinky displayed them in her study and used a magnifying glass to scrutiny the photos in detail.

After one hour…

"Bingo, here it is. A prudent discovery indeed," Rinky spoke to herself in delight.

She then walked towards the kitchen where her mom was instructing the cook.

"Mom, can you pack me a light lunch. I will go to the gym, and then have something before visiting Dimple's house."

"Yes I can. You change and get ready, meanwhile I will pack something light."

Rinky was up and ready by 15 minutes and rushed outside with the lunch box. Mrs. Khanna smiled, she knew her daughter is due to crack the puzzle.

At the gym, Rinky met Vicky. She continued with her regular training schedule for about 30 minutes and then stopped.

"Hey Vicky, did Archana have multiple boyfriends. I mean, did she ever come to the gym with them or maybe only one person," Rinky tried to be as casual as possible.

"I think I told you I do not indulge in the personal matters of my clients," Vicky replied in a serious tone, unwillingly answering to her query.

"Oh no, I am not saying that. I am just asking a question, whether you have ever noticed, that's all."

"No I have not. By the way, I will be out of town for few days so you may have to continue your training with the other instructors. Also I need to leave in few minutes, have an appointment in the city."

Rinky nodded and spoke, "So where are you going? Is it some other assignment? And are you visiting friends in the city?"

"You ask too many questions. Yes some other assignment and yes visiting friends. Happy?"

"Sorry sorry, I was just curious."

Vicky glanced at Rinky once, and then started walking towards the shower and changing rooms. Rinky waited for sometime and the moment he was out of sight, she quickly walked towards the pillar near the gym entrance and exit door, and hid herself from anyone's view.

After 15 minutes, she noticed Vicky approaching the door. He was not in his usual full sleeves shirt and trousers, but in a rugged jeans and a sleeveless t-shirt. Rinky noticed a tattoo in his right hand covering the muscles. Somehow she zoomed in her mobile camera and tried to capture his image.

Rinky glanced at her watch. It was 2:30 PM. She quickly took a shower in the gym, changed, and went to the cafeteria to finish off her lunch. By 3:15 PM, she moved out of the gym, booked a cab to reach Dimple's house.

Dimple's facial expression seemed not very convincing on meeting Rinky.

"Please sit and can you make it fast. I need to go out," Dimple insisted.

"Sure, I am sorry. It's just a few queries. Did Ms Archana share all her secrets with you. I mean if you can share some interesting facts, you know my article will be bit attractive. Else plain simple stories are not enticing, if you can understand," Rinky completed and gulped down.

"I don't know if she shared all are secrets with me. What exactly you want to know?"

"It can be anything Ms Dimple. Boyfriends, any interesting incident or trip."

Dimple sighed. "Yes she had, not sure if they can be termed as boyfriends as I think she never went for any serious relationships, except one."

Rinky was curious, "Except one? Who was it? Anything special?"

"Ah! Well, it's not that Archana was serious but the guy was as per my predictions. She never wanted to settle down in life, like get married and children etc. She was ambitious and was adamant about her career. Like all other guys, she considered this particular guy under the same category. But then later it seemed she developed a special fascination towards the guy which was a bit odd and unbelievable. Her conversations about the guy changed and her outstation visits also increased. But then as usual after few such visits, she went into few untoward encounters which eventually paved the way for a break-up. They went on multiple trips, and I have heard those were super lavish ones."

"Any reason Ms Dimple, for the break-up."

"Yeah as per Archana, the guy wanted to marry and then settle down which did not gel with her at all. And it seems the guy was a bit possessive and did not want to get off her. So she had to struggle and juggle a bit for a "the end" to the relationship."

"You say the guy was possessive. Did he easily leave her, or did he continue pursuing her?"

"Hey come on, enough. I told you what I knew. She had the power, the money, and connects. How long can a petty guy confront her? Eventually he had to succumb. And that exactly was the guy's fate. That's all, I do not desire to prolong this discussion anymore."

"Understand Ms Dimple. Understand you do not want to prolong the discussion. But what if I say, your friend was killed, she did not commit suicide. Will you be ok with it?" Rinky knew she had to use her weapon and she did it.

"What? Archana was killed? Who are you? And why are you saying this? Police had informed us that she committed suicide? Are you from the police?" Dimple's face was red, her voice almost trembling.

Rinky went near her, "You loved your friend right. She was your bestie. You knew she was ambitious and was focused on her career. Just now you told me she did not want to marry and settle down. How on earth then she will think to commit suicide? Have you ever thought about it? You just believed what the police had to say and decided to just grief about her death. What kind of a friend are you?"

Dimple was shivering and started sobbing.

"Trust me Ms Dimple. I am a well-wisher of Ms Archana. You will know who I am eventually. But as a trusted friend, if you want to decode how and why Archana got killed, then please help me, cooperate with me to decipher the truth. Will you?"

Dimple controlled herself, wiped her tears and replied, "I will."

"Thanks, then please tell me about this affair. What all you know about it."

So Dimple started.

"It was a Saturday and on every weekend Archana devoted considerable amount of time for her workouts. The day before we had planned for a brunch and hence we were to meet at about 11:30 AM in one of the restaurants near her home. When we met, she was super charged and excited. I was happy for her and on asking her the reason, she explained meeting a person at a party. She spoke about him a lot, seemed handsome and good looking and was a fitness freak like her. Though I knew she can never be serious, yet as a bestie I always listened to her. She had already planned some trips with him, and meet ups etc.

The relationship continued. She used to go for trips abroad with him and never hesitated to spend luxuriously. I did warn her sometimes and requested to check whether the guy was in sync with her mentality and thoughts, since I know she can never be serious in relation. She ignored me, just swayed in it. And she eventually faced the consequence. The guy wanted to marry her and kept on insisting on it. I think he started blackmailing her. She was very much disturbed those days and kept indoors mostly. Even I was not invited inside the house. She cancelled many of her shoots, films, and events. One day, she just vanished suddenly for a trip to Maldives. She came back after a month. I tried a lot to find out what was wrong with her, whether she was in trouble. But she never revealed anything, just said she wanted to keep this one thing as a secret. She never spoke about that guy after returning from her trip. She was an influential lady, I felt she had taken up some measures to stop the guy from disturbing her."

Dimple paused.

"Can you tell me approximately the date when Ms Archana traveled to Maldives?" Rinky questioned.

"Yes I do. It was sometime in June last year."

Rinky opened up her mobile phone, searched for the photo she had taken of Archana's pregnancy tests and the prescription.

"See this Ms Dimple, check the date on these reports and prescriptions. The dates are almost matching. Ms Archana was pregnant, no one knew about it not even you. And I am not forging the data. I never knew the date until you told me few minutes back. Yet the dates are almost matching."

"Oh God ! Is this why she was so troubled? What happened to the baby? Oh you mean to say she went to Maldives for abortion. She went there just to avoid the prying eyes of the media. I am able to connect the dots now. But then why will someone kill her? Oh no, is it the guy," Dimple started shivering again.

"It can be. It looks like the guy was possessive and must have been forced maybe by some wrong means to leave Ms Archana. I have a strong feeling he took revenge. If that is true, the big question is who the guy is and how did he kill her," Rinky sighed, yet her eyes were bright, seemed she was in track.

"Who are you? Are you a private detective?"

"Yes I am. But you cannot mention this to anyone for now. If you do that, we will lose the opportunity of finding out who the killer is. I hope you understand."

"I do, and what do I call you as? Is it Rinky or is it your fake name like most detectives"

Rinky smiled, "No its Rinky only, you can call me by this name. Now can you tell me who are the people she used to meet and which places she frequented often within the city?"

"I will try to tell you everything I know about Archana, Rinky. She loved attention and if anyone did so she used to cling with that person till the time she felt she was comfortable. The moment she was fed up or bored or was overwhelmed, she just drifted away from that person. It's only the guy with whom she became overly intimate. We both were exceptions though, Tony and I, maybe because we were professionally connected with her. I don't know if she had developed any special friendship with anyone other than that guy, though she would rattle out about everyone in front of me. I considered those relationships as casual as her words had no seriousness in them."

"But Ms Dimple, in any of your conversations with her, did you feel she was close with anyone else? Maybe she spoke more about that person in comparison to others. Try to think please, its important."

"Yes I am trying to. I think there were two persons, one she praised a lot and one is that guy she spoke about him passionately many a times."

"Who is that other person, Ms Dimple?" Rinky's face brightened.

"The other was the gym guy she used to train with. But those were just praises, how he helped her in her diet and her physical fitness. Though I have seldom seen her praising someone especially a person who is not even an inch similar to her stature, hence you can consider her over superfluous glorifications as unusual."

"I see. Do you know his name, by any chance or seen his photographs?"

"Yes I think, his name is Vicky, if I remember correctly. She had once shown a photograph in the gym, I vaguely recollect though."

Rinky opened up her phone again, "Is this the guy?"

Dimply stared attentively at the photo, "Yes the face looks similar. Can't be sure 100%, yet seems to be."

Rinky nodded, her face was stern.

"Tell me something about the guy she was close with, more details I meant," Rinky said.

"The guy was a hotel chain owner, he had hotels in India and abroad. Seems he was quite well off, owned cars and expensive dresses and accessories. No doubt she was attracted towards him, at par with her reputation and status."

"Do you have any photographs of him?"

"No Rinky. But Archana had shown me his photos in her mobile. But most of them were not clear, face was mostly dark. She was worried about being noticed with this guy and then the media chasing her."

"Her mobile is with the police right?" Rinky asked.

"Yes I suppose. They took away I think, the day when she died," Dimple's voice sounded heavy.

Rinky placed her comforting hand on Dimple's shoulders, "Let me try to get hold of her phone. Did the police not enquire about her relations with other people etc. You know what I mean right, the way I am asking."

"No Rinky, they did not. After few days of investigation, they just concluded she committed suicide."

"That's another strange part. I am sensing some foul play. Is there any chance of retrieving the handwriting of the hotelier, meaning some paper he had left with Archana where we can check?" Rinky enquired.

"No as far as I remember, maybe Archana had but since I have never met the person nor did he visit us in Mumbai I don't recollect any paper as such where we can check his handwriting. May I ask the reason for asking?"

"I was able to check some letters hidden in her wardrobe, written by some guy who was close with her. We could have tried to match the handwriting. By the way do you know Anu well enough?"

"Anu, the girl whom Archana recruited as a PA kind of?"

"Yes, correct."

"But how do you know her? What I meant is, she was just an employee, not a personality to be noticed and spoken about."

"Ms Dimple, I think you are forgetting something. I am a private detective and a professional. For me everyone is a suspect."

"Am I not a suspect then, Rinky?"

"You were, but now you are not and I am 100% accurate in that," Rinky smiled sarcastically.

"Ok, but then how come you are trusting me?"

"I think I am correct in my action. I started investigating because Anu called me and requested me to intervene even though police had closed the case from their end as a suicide."

"What, Anu? Unbelievable? How on earth she felt that it cannot be a suicide? She was just a normal employee, assisting her in her schedules, meetings etc."

"It surprised me too, Ms Dimple. An ordinary person is so much confident about her employer's death as not suicide. Does she suspect anyone and is not able to confide the name to the police? And maybe if she does, she may be in danger. Or she is herself guilty in this case. So there are lot of possibilities. Did you notice any unusual behaviour in her, ever?"

"That will be difficult to say. I never noticed her so carefully. Her interactions were mostly with Archana. She was an obedient employee and as far as I know, Archana never had any problems with her work."

"My only problem is I am investigating this case unofficially. I do not have access to all the assets of Ms Archana," Rinky again sighed.

"Can we not request the police to reopen the case and investigate, saying we feel there must be some foul play. We can try to convince them that Archana is not a person to commit suicide. She had work lined up and was super ambitious."

"It's a tough one, only if you can help," Rinky answered and looked straight into the eyes of Dimple.

"What do I have to do, tell me?" Dimple asked.

"I know a high-ranking officer in the CID. We will fix an appointment with him. He will not rely on me to speak with the local police and re-open the case or hand over to CID. If you speak and plead him as her bestie, then it may work. Only we both have to act as if we are close friends and know each other for long. Are you ok with this plan?" Rinky was eager to receive a positive answer.

After a minute's pause, Dimple replied, "I am ok. Let's do it."

Rinky felt relieved, "Thank you so much, Ms Dimple. Wait for my call tomorrow. I will let you know when and where to meet, we have to do this fast."

After bidding bye, Rinky left for her home. Her effort clicked, she could gain the trust and confidence of Dimple. This is exactly what she wanted, though the path was still tough to overcome. But atleast there was some light in her analysis. Her next sprint was to contact the State Crime Investigation Department, and connect with her mentor and her father's friend Mr. Ahluwahlia. He was the Special Inspector General of Police in CID and the person whom Rinky needed the most at this hour.

She informed her mother and Rishav about contacting Mr Ahluwahlia and they both gave her an assurance nod which was a boost for her.

Sensible Plan

"Hey Rinky, my brave, smart and sweet doll. How are you?"

Rinky loved this voice, the person she admired and was her idol in her journey till now.

"I am good and how are you Ahluwalia uncle?" Rinky spoke out.

"I am good, my dear. But as you know, it's my duty hours now. Can we speak later in the evening?"

"I am sorry uncle. I know you are busy now. But this is very urgent. Can I somehow meet you today, it's about an importance case I have forcefully tangled myself. You are the only person who can assist me," Rinky pleaded.

"Seems an issue. I have a slot free between 1 PM to 2 PM at the lunch time. You have to manage within it."

"Sure sure uncle. Thanks a lot. I will be there with my friend sharp at 1 PM," Rinky was delighted.

"Ok Ok let's see what my smart girl is into. Till then take care and bye," Mr Ahluwalia hung up the phone.

Rinky knew she cannot afford to miss this opportunity, her golden chance to reopen the case. She called up Dimple, and mentioned the time slot she received from Mr Ahluwalia. And as promised at 1 PM, she was at the State Crime Investigation Department office accompanied by Dimple. Mr Ahluwalia's PA was already aware of their arrival, hence ushered them to step inside his office once they arrived.

"Hello, here comes my smart girl". As soon as Rinky stepped inside, Mr Ahluwalia stood up, greeted and hugged her.

"Uncle, glad I could meet you. I tried my best this time to resolve the case through my own sources, but stuck now at a crucial junction, which I cannot wade across without your guidance and support."

"Hey my girl, no hesitation. You know how special you are for me. Now sit down and speak out."

"Oops sorry my bad. Uncle, this is Dimple. Actually it's due to her plea and request, I have taken up this case."

"Glad to meet you, Sir". Dimple shook hands with Mr Ahluwalia, in exchange received a warm smile.

"Ya so now you have exactly 1 hour, go on Rinky," Mr Ahluwalia sat down in his chair. Without any further delay, Rinky related the whole incident.

"What an insane act, Rinky? You could have atleast consulted with me before deciding to investigate such a high profile case which is closed and is so sensitive. And I must scold your mother for not even warning you."

"I am sorry uncle, I should have consulted you. But somehow, both me and Mom were somehow convinced of some foul play and wanted to dive into it. I know its sort of immaturity on my part, but the smell of mystery just dragged me into it."

"Understand my Braveheart girl," Mr Ahluwalia then turned sternly at Dimple, "And yes Miss, how come you are so sure that Ms Archana did not commit suicide? And why were you silent before? What made you contact a private investigator and not police?"

Rinky could sense the nervousness in Dimple. She knew Mr Ahluwalia wont accept the bluff easily.

"Pardon her, uncle. She was afraid of being accused and was so shocked by the death that she was not sure how to act."

"Hmm, but Rinky. The case cannot be re-opened, that's against the ethics. But if you can provide me substantial evidence and find out the accused within 2 days, then I will take a chance. But remember, the evidence have to be convincing and accurate. Else you have to forget the case forever."

"Done, Uncle."

"Great, go ahead young lady. Let me see how smart my girl is," Mr Ahluwalia returned back a smile.

In 5 minutes, Rinky and Dimple exited the Crime department office.

"I need to collect my thoughts, Dimple. Each and every second is now crucial for me. Though uncle said the case is closed, I think it's not and the 2 days is the hint for it. In all cases, the Crime department keeps a buffer before permanently closing the case. So, I have to hurry."

"How can I help you, Rinky?" Dimple's voice sounded confused.

"You go home, Dimple. I need to speak to this Vicky guy, maybe he knows something which he is not sharing with me. We need to find out the other guy, maybe he is linked to Archana's death. I have a sense Vicky knows that guy, seems Archana had confided in him and hence Vicky is not willing to share all the information with me. You go home now, I will call you if I need you."

Having said this, Rinky left for her home and on her way called up Rishav.

"Rishav, were you able to trace Vicky and Archana?"

"Yes, I was about to call you. They are in a bike and heading towards Juhu beach. You also start immediately, am already in pursuit with one of my guys. If they stop somewhere, I will message you the location."

"Alright Rishav, I am starting now."

Rinky booked an uber and was on her way. After 20 mins, she received the location from Rishav. It was a café near the beach. It took her another 10 mins to reach the location.

"Rishav, hope they are still in the café?"

"Yes, hurry up."

They both barged into the café and noticed both of them sitting down at a far end corner, at an isolated area inside the café.

"Hi Anu, Hi Vicky, oops I did not know you both are friends, sorry am I right? Or partners? Or husband wife?" Rinky had a sarcastic smile on her.

Anu almost jumped up from her seat, startled, "Vicky? His name is Jose? And how do you know him?"

Vicky did not speak a word. Rinky noticed he was gulping within himself and took a deep breath too.

"Well, what a coincidence. Vicky is one of the instructors in the gym I go to. And surprisingly he was Ms Archana's instructor too. And Anu, you came to me to investigate Archana's sudden death. Wondering how come there is a linkage?"

"Maam's instructor? You work in a gym? I am confused, what's going on?" Anu's face was red.

"Anu, my name is Jose only. I don't know what this lady is talking about," Vicky spoke up and then looked sternly at Rinky, "Hey Miss, how come you are interfering in our personal space. Buzz off."

"Chill, Vicky. I am a private investigator and I have some professional agreement with Anu. I am investigating a case on her request and by virtue of it, I am authorized to suspect anyone. So you are also in my suspect list. Now stop pointing your fingers towards me and sit down."

"You lied about your name and profession? What should I call you Jose Branco or Vicky? Oh my God, I was fooled," Anu's voice was shivering.

"Calm down, Anu. I think you were right in approaching me to investigate the death. I think Vicky knows things which he has not shared till now."

"You cannot force me to speak here. And I am leaving right now," Vicky attempted to stand. But Rishav forced him to sit.

"Hey Hey, you are dealing with the Police. So shut your mouth and sit down. If you try to act smart, consequences may be worse," Rishav's voice was stern.

Vicky sat down reluctantly, his head down.

"Now, will you speak up, Vicky. What was your relation with Ms Archana? Why did you pair up with Anu and not reveal your identity to her? You took leave from gym and spent time with Anu, bluffing that you had a hotel business at Goa," Rinky started questioning.

She continued.. "You cannot escape anymore. Anyhow Anu is going to report against you with the police for false identity and the moment police starts investigating, you will be caught for the guilt which you are trying to hide. So speak up."

"Speak up, you moron. What did you do with Maam?" Anu was furious.

"Anu, can I do the talking please?" Rinky insisted. Anu nodded in agreement.

"Come on, now speak," Rishav pulled a chair and sat in front of him.

Vicky sighed a deep breath again, "So my life ends here, just because I loved someone and wanted to have a family with kids." He started sobbing.

Rinky poured water in a glass and handed over to Vicky, "Here, have some water. See Vicky, if you speak the truth then we may try to help you. But if you hide then fate will take its due course."

"My fate is gone. Listen then. I never owned a hotel business, but I had been working in a hotel "Sonam Bay" in Goa as a manager. It's not a 5-star hotel but a 3-star hotel and I was happy with my work. My boss, Joel Gonsalves, the owner of the hotel, was also good. My sole aim in life was to be good at work and then eventually find a suitable partner, get married and raise a family. Everything was going on smoothly and then that fatal day. I call it fatal, because after that day my life changed," Vicky said.

"Sonam Bay and Joel Gonsalves. Remember the names, Rishav?"

"Yes I do, Rinky. Dots are connecting."

"What happened on that day?" Rinky turned towards Vicky and was curious.

"My boss was a smart guy, not very good-looking but had a special aura to charm the ladies. We had a frequent guest in our hotel and that was Ms Archana. We all knew she was famous. My boss himself wanted to specially take care of her comfort and as usual went ahead with his flirting behaviour. Somehow Ms Archana fell in that trap and started enjoying the attention. She was supposed to check out the next day, but she did not. She extended her stay, and spent ample time with my boss. She seemed to be enjoying her company and on the other hand my boss had nothing for it, just a mere time-pass. I tried to convey the message many a times to her but could not. The relationship continued and I was asked not to speak about it anywhere, else I may lose my job and maybe suffer consequences more than that. Afraid, I kept quiet. Their physical intimacy increased day by day, they went to places together and all the expenses were born by Ms Archana. My boss took complete advantage of her fame and money."

As Vicky was narrating, Dimple stepped in to the hotel. Rinky had called her, since she felt witnesses were important to solve the case. Also she wanted to check the dates of Archana's travels, as mentioned by Vicky, with Dimple for authenticity and alignment.

Vicky continued… "Somehow the uneasiness of Ms Archana being fooled was eating me day by day. I was always on the look out for a chance to approach her and reveal the wicked motive of my boss. And one day I did get a chance. My boss had to leave for a family marriage party and Ms Archana was a bit drunk. Boss had given me special instructions to take care of her needs as he did not rely on anyone else and was worried that she may blabber out something in her drunken state. At about 10 PM I took her order for dinner and knocked at her room. She opened the door and ushered me to come inside. I have to swear, she was looking drop dead gorgeous without make up and without any lavish dress. I kept the dinner on the table and stood there. The moment she asked if I had to say something, I just spoke about my boss's intentions. She was quiet for few minutes and then started crying profusely. I controlled myself for few seconds and then I was holding her in my arms. She held me tight and I did the same. We were grippingly close to each other, felt each other's breath and I realized how beautiful she was. Our lips touched each other and we went into a deep kiss. It was relentless and we were unstoppable. We did everything, that night was our night, such passion and such closeness."

Vicky stopped for a second and Rinky saw all eyes staring towards him in surprise. She felt sorry for Anu, her face pale in being diched.

"Next morning when we were both in our senses, Ms Archana was terrified. She literally pleaded me to keep it secret and it was completely an accident. I had to agree but I knew I was not following my heart. My emotions and my feelings were unable to term it as an accident. Days went, she left the hotel and then came back again, each time lazing out with my boss. I used to burn from inside, tried many times to be near her but she just ignored me. One day, it was my duty to serve the dinner in her room where my boss was also present. As I approached the room, I heard loud voices of both. The gist of the heated discussion was, Ms Archana was pregnant, she wanted to keep the baby, get married to my boss and be family. My boss's reply was he always used protection while being physically intimate with Archana and hence the baby cannot belong to him. He started accusing Archana of sleeping with many men. In few minutes, my boss barged out of the room in anger and I could hear Archana sobbing inside. I stepped inside the room and kept the dinner at the table. Archana looked up, was furious and just asked me to leave. I was about to leave but stopped and asked a question – When did you realize you are pregnant? She was stunned and said angrily – I am not pregnant, what the hell are you talking about? Leave the room. I asked her – Do you remember we had sex? On hearing this, she became more furious – You idiot, how dare you? Just because I was drunk that day, you felt you can say anything. Nothing happened, now get lost."

There was silence as Vicky spoke, none interfered.

Vicky went on.. "I bowed down my head and started walking towards the door. Then I stopped and turned towards her – That baby is ours. I am ready to marry you, we can have a beautiful family together. – There was rage in her eyes – How dare you? Look at yourself, do you know with whom you are speaking with? If you do not leave the room, I will be forced to call my security – I left the room."

"How come you were so sure about the baby?" Rinky asked.

Vicky smiled, "My boss was impotent. I knew all his secrets. So I was sure."

"So what happened after that?" Rishav asked.

"Archana could not return back to the hotel as her reputation was at stake, she being pregnant. My boss sold off the hotel and just vanished. I could not trace her whereabouts for long, but I had to because of my child. I was eager to know whether it was a boy or a girl and somehow I was desperate to convince Archana about my fatherhood. I decided to go to Mumbai and check with her. I knew she wont entertain me so

I thought of a plan. I had to find out about her life, her travels, her schedules etc. So I had to trap Archana, that was the easiest way for me. From her I checked the gym Archana frequented and took a job there after some forging of certificates and experience. The day we met she was unable to recognize me as I had my beard on and muscles on. But when I revealed myself, she was again furious. But I gained her confidence by not mentioning about her pregnancy or the baby. Just focused on being friends and helping her in her fitness regime. I was successful, she was happy in my company and we started spending ample time with each other. After sufficient gap, I casually asked about the child. And then I received the most shocking news. She had gone to Maldives and had aborted the child as she could not ruin her reputation. I was shocked – she killed my baby. She was a murderer, she just killed my baby, my innocent baby. How could she? And you know what, a murderer is deserved to die. So I slowly started poisoning her, with the medicines and nutrients. And one day the murderer was killed."

"You killed Archana, oh my God," Dimple exclaimed.

"That's not killing, that's punishment. She had killed my child, so she had to be punished. I punished her, I am a true father to my child." Vicky started laughing like an insane person.

"Why the hell are you still spending time with me then?" Anu was stunned.

"You are my warrior in this mission, I am obliged towards you. To express my gratitude to you, I am here," Vicky spoke.

"Oh God, you are a sick person," Anu started sobbing.

Rinky held Anu and comforted her, and looked towards Vicky, "But how did you manage to provide her the dosage of Paraquat. Medicines are prescribed by doctors and when I enquired from her doctor, he only spoke about her sleeping pills and nothing else."

"Remember I mentioned about our intimate physical relation. We did many times here in Mumbai and even in Goa. And I successfully convinced her that she needed medicines to charge up her sexual energy. She fell prey to that and I gave her the dreadful poison. She killed my baby, my small baby, she deserved to die."

"Rinky, he is not normal. I have recorded what he had spoken so far," Rishav spoke.

"Thanks Rishav, while you keep him in custody, I need to hurry and present the evidence to Ahluwalia uncle. Let the case be reopened as fast as possible," Rinky replied.

"Sure Rinky, unbelievable fate indeed."

"Anu, its entirely because of you the case was resolved. Else who knows, similar incident might have happened with you too. Come with me as the Crime department must know about your smart act in the investigation. Without you, it would have been just a suicide case. And Dimple thanks for trusting me else uncle would not have granted permission to continue with the investigation," Rinky hugged both Anu and Dimple.

That day, Rinky handed over the evidence to Mr Ahluwalia, Vicky was arrested and immediately taken to a mental asylum. Anu decided to change her job and leave the city. Tony too called up Rinky after hearing the details from Dimple.

Rishav had accompanied Rinky throughout. "By the way Rinky, one thing I could not understand – Dimple had mentioned about Ms Archana speaking in length about one guy with whom she was serious. Was it Joel or Vicky? And as per Vicky, Archana wanted to keep the baby but Joel was not interested. Somehow I am not able to link."

"Archana was a clever lady, and we never know whether she wanted to have the baby or she was furious with Joel and wanted to punish him. She will never mention about Vicky passionately considering her fame and reputation. Definitely she did want to have the baby and was unable to bear the fact that someone could overpower her and make her pregnant. Or she understood the baby was from Vicky and was again unable to bear the fact that she slept and had sex with an ordinary person who made her pregnant. I feel she lost her mind, being controlled by two guys, quite contrary to her personality. But she was severely hypnotized later by Vicky in the gym and fell prey to him which is an irony. But she was complicated too, painted a different image of hers and her lovers in front of Dimple, sort of fooled her too," Rinky explained.

"Hmm, now I can understand. Truly a complex situation. By the way Maam congratulations for solving the case and catching the real culprit," Rishav hugged Rinky.

Rinky smiled and then bid goodbye to him and went back home.

At home…

"Mom, my first case as a private investigator. Such eventful, at each moment I felt I should quit. But your encouragement and a sheer determination within me worked."

"Yes dear, I am delighted. And yes more to come."

"Yup Mommy dear. Rinky is ready." And they both cuddled on to each other.

About the Author

Kuntala Bhattacharya

Kuntala, is an established IT consultant, writer, poet, and blogger.

Her articles, short stories, and poems have been published on many websites and have been appreciated by readers. She has authored several books, a mix of novels, short stories and poems.

Born and brought up in West Bengal, she always had a special fascination for literature. Her writing ventures in minimalistic form started from her college days. And then it continued to expand vividly, increasing her zeal to venture into the world of writers and poets.

Throughout her professional life, she has ventured into different places and interacted with people from different facets of life. Her innumerable experiences are reflected in her writings.

She likes using simple words for the benefit of readers of all generations. Her flow of words is smooth, often deliberating on the intrinsic aspects of the plot. She believes it is necessary to engage the readers at every moment in a story, without letting them indulge into a feeling of boredom.

You can connect with her at :

1. *https://instagram.com/travelogue.of.kuntala* OR

2. *https://www.facebook.com/travelogueunlimited* OR

3. *Visit her website https://travelogueofkuntala.com*